ALSO BY RON HANSEN

FICTION
Isn't It Romantic?

Hitler's Niece

Atticus

Mariette in Ecstasy

Nebraska

The Assassination of Jesse James
by the Coward Robert Ford

Desperadoes

ESSAYS
A Stay Against Confusion: Essays on Faith and Fiction

FOR CHILDREN
The Shadowmaker

AS EDITOR
You've Got to Read This: Contemporary American Writers
Introduce Stories That Held Them in Awe
(with Jim Shepard)

You Don't Know What Love Is:
Contemporary American Short Stories

EXILES

EXILES

RON HANSEN

FARRAR, STRAUS AND GIROUX

NEW YORK

Farrar, Straus and Giroux
18 West 18th Street, New York 10011

Distributed in Canada by Douglas & McIntyre Ltd.
Printed in the United States of America
First edition, 2008

Library of Congress Cataloging-in-Publication Data
Hansen, Ron, 1947–
    Exiles / Ron Hansen. — 1st ed.
        p.   cm
    ISBN-13: 978-0-374-15097-6 (hardcover : alk. paper)
    ISBN-10: 0-374-15097-4 (hardcover : alk. paper)
    1. Hopkins, Gerard Manley, 1844–1889—Fiction.   2. Hopkins, Gerard
Manley, 1844–1889. Wreck of the Deutschland—Fiction.   3. Poets,
English—19th century—Fiction.   4. Jesuits—England—Fiction.   I. Title.

PS3558.A5133E95 2008
813'.54—dc22

                                                            2007046836

Designed by Jonathan D. Lippincott

www.fsgbooks.com

1   3   5   7   9   10   8   6   4   2

To Joseph J. Feeney, S.J., Paul Mariani,
and all my friends in the Society of Jesus

CONTENTS

AUTHOR'S NOTE

This is a work of fiction based on fact. Because my protagonists are not wholly invented, I have felt a duty to their memories, and whenever there were holes in my information about them, such as often happened with the five little-known nuns who died in the shipwreck, I have sought similarities in the memoirs of other European religious in the nineteenth century. With Hopkins himself, a great deal more background was available and the novelist's function became that of making dramatic what is otherwise contained in Hopkins's letters and journals. Care has been taken not to contradict biographical details or historical testimony, but the characters finally represent my own interpretation of people who actually lived more than a century ago.

EXILES

I

HOPKINS IN WALES

Wednesday, December 8th, 1875. A soft confetti of snow-flakes was fluttering down upon Wales. The higher window-panes were gardens of frost. His right hand still twined a rosary, its anesthetic routine of prayers his nightly defense against sleeplessness. Lying in bed in his nightshirt and black woolen stockings, Hopkins recited his Morning Offering, then stood to use the chamber pot. The scuttle contained only a scarcity of coals and he would want those for his studies, so he gashed the fireplace embers with an iron poker and held his hands over their golden, waning heat. He lit and chim-neyed one gas retort on the wall.

Washing with Castile soap and icy water, he worried over his scrawniness, his spindle shins, the green yarns of vein in his forearms, his face so thin that his zygomatic bones and jaw shaped harps underneath his ginger-brown, one-inch beard and mustache. His high school nickname was Skin, and even now at age thirty-one he weighed hardly a hundred pounds, with a jockey's height of five foot four. "Eats like a parakeet," Cyprian Splaine had said just last night, and Rickaby joked, "Eats like a *single* keet."

Yesterday's long underwear would do, Hopkins thought, and then a jersey that the Jesuit Theologate's laundress had shrunk. Over them he buttoned a cuff-frayed and graying black cassock with its faint stink of him, waisted it with a hand-wide black cincture, snapped on a starched white Roman collar, and laced on his ankle-high black walking shoes. And then he dipped a horsehair toothbrush in a yellow box of bicarbonate of soda and assaulted his grimace in the spotted mirror hanging over the washstand, amusing himself by rhyming: *Gerardus M. Hopkins, S.J. / Auditor Theologiae. / Here at Saint Beuno's. / Far too long, my nose.*

•

Because December 8th was the Catholic solemnity of the Immaculate Conception of Mary, classes were canceled and the forty-one seminarians and ten professors at Saint Beuno's School of Theology could while away the wide hours of morning and afternoon in holy obedience to hobbies and exercise in the glens and pastures of northern Wales.

Eight played football on a slanted pitch, in jerseys and cardigans, their hands shoved deep into their woolen trouser pockets due to the rawness of wind and cold. Bill Dubberley and three others went down to the green River Elwy with rods and reels "to do," as they announced at breakfast, "evil things to the fish." A professor of ecclesiology strolled outside in his derby, overcoat, cassock, and calabash pipe, reading his breviary. Edward Reeve stayed inside and tried to teach parlor tricks to his snappish pet ferret with white crumbles of Yorkshire cheese. Three Brothers worked noisily in the kitchen, preparing the one p.m. dinner, as Frank Scoles, a newly ordained priest, baked an angel food cake. Clement

Barraud scowled with the world's own confusion as he read a gift copy of *The Temptation of Saint Anthony*, by Gustave Flaubert, that the Rector had given him permission to keep. A pianist of exemplary patience was in the sacristy practicing Johann Sebastian Bach's minuets on the grunting harmonium there. And Hopkins invited with him on a ramble to the city of Saint Asaph, three miles north, Joseph Rickaby, a very smart runt with an M.A. in philosophy who was the son of the butler to Lord Herries, and Albert Wagner, the "t" not sounded, a shy, smiling man from the Province of Lyons in France whose seniority in the Society of Jesus would cause him to be the first in their second-year class to be ordained a priest.

Strolling to Saint Asaph, Rickaby mentioned a variety of writing projects that he wanted to tackle once examinations were concluded and was particularly keen on getting started on an index to the works of John Henry Newman. Wagner was a sterling linguist who said his post-examination project was to learn Coptic as a prelude to the study of Egyptian. Whereas Hopkins claimed he had no grand ambitions for the holidays; that the pursuit of holiness was enough.

Rickaby said, "But I'm scandalized you would lie so flagrantly on one of Our Lady's feasts! You're a hobbyist if I've ever seen one. Always learning Welsh, hunting etymologies, sketching cloud formations . . ."

". . . enduring contradictions."

"But hobbies are excellent things!" Rickaby said. "A project is like a sponge that sucks up all your attention and keeps you from brooding over whatever displeases you. Some overriding interest is the great preservative against quarreling and mutinous thoughts."

Hopkins smiled. "I'm having a mutinous thought just now."

Rickaby turned to Wagner. "Restless as a weevil, our gentle Hop is. Don't think he won't fill his hours with something."

The theologians carried sandwiches but no coins, and the city of Saint Asaph was without great fascination, so they simply visited the once-Catholic cathedral to see the restoration of the intricately wood-carved choir stalls that Oliver Cromwell tried to destroy by using them as cattle pens. And then the three walked back to Saint Beuno's in the sifting snow, edifying each other by praying the five glorious mysteries of the Rosary on the way, and then goading the scholastics fishing the Elwy until Bill Dubberley caught a trout and fell waist deep in the river while hauling it in.

Hopkins shouted, "Has it *dampened* your enthusiasm, Bill?"

A jubilant Dubberley hoisted his trout.

To his father, Hopkins would write that on the Elwy "there is good fishing for those who do not see that after bad fishing the next worst thing is good fishing."

•

At six the whole school went to the main chapel in their cassocks and birettas for the singing of Vespers and for the Benediction and Exposition of the Blessed Sacrament, Rector James Jones, the celebrant, incensing the congregation and the Host, leading them in the Eucharistic hymn *"Tantum Ergo,"* and blessing them with the ceremonial monstrance, in which the Host seemed the core of golden rays of sunlight.

And then, to honor the solemnity at the evening supper, a quart decanter of claret was on each refectory table in addition to the usual pitcher of ale. Conversation in English was allowed, so there was a good deal of laughter, and the priests and scholastics lingered until Brother Fogherty shouted, "Are you all still dithering here?" and shooed them out so he could stack the Windsor chairs and wet-mop the oak floor.

Exiting the room, Reverend Josef Floeck of Germany, a professor of dogmatic theology who had recently been ostracized with other Jesuits by Otto von Bismarck, asked Hopkins, "Haff you read about za *Deutschland* und za fife German nuns?"

•

Hopkins went to a scholastics' recreation room that was as large and high-ceilinged as some village churches, but furnished like a run-down gentlemen's club, with a variety of Irish Georgian wingback chairs surrounding a great fireplace, two walnut secretaries for writing, each with something wrong with it, hand-me-down upholstered sofas and library chairs, a green felt billiards table, and card tables for whist or the game that Americans called checkers, the English called draughts, and Albert Wagner called *le jeu plaisant de dames*.

Wednesday morning's London *Times* was still cool from its afternoon journey from Rhyl as Hopkins carried it to a sofa underneath a sconced gas retort. The front page, as always, was filled with three- and four-line advertisements for Newcastle, Silkstone, or Wall's-End coal, Bailey's elastic stockings, ladies' abdominal belts, Pulvermacher's Patent Galvanic Chain Bands, Antakos corn plasters, Iceland Liniment for chilblains, and "Want Places" appeals from wet nurses, scullery maids, and cooks, each willing to supply testimonials about their skills and finer qualities. Other pages reported the

meteorological data for the month of November, and news
from Berlin about Britain's shrewd purchase of shares in the
Suez Canal. Writing from Rome was an "occasional correspondent" who noted Italy's sarcastic response to the contempt for Catholicism of Britain's former Prime Minister,
William Gladstone, who'd written that the Jesuits in particular were "the deadliest foes that mental and moral liberty
have ever known." Old news for Hopkins, and he lost interest in the article after the first paragraph. But on page 5, next
to a dull column on President Ulysses S. Grant's address to
the Congress of the United States, was a headline, LOSS OF
THE DEUTSCHLAND.

"Wrecks and Casualties" was a regular department in
each issue of *The Times*—sixteen accidents were recorded on
December 8th—and among the Victorians there was a general fascination with tales of great tragedies at sea. But more
than that, Hopkins's father was the author of *A Handbook of
Average* and *A Manual of Marine Insurance*, both standard
reference books for negotiating, averaging, and adjusting the
liabilities to insurance underwriters of cargo losses and shipwrecks, so Hopkins grew up in a world wet with marine accidents and was especially attentive to them.

In this instance, telegrams from Sheerness, Harwich, and
the Lords of the Admiralty were pieced together with a Press
Association report, each duplicating or elaborating on the
news that the North German Lloyd steamer *Deutschland*,
heading to New York from the port of Bremen in a heavy
gale, ran aground on a sandbank near the mouth of the
Thames River at five in the morning on December 6th. "She
afterwards knocked over the sand, and is now lying in 4½
fathoms, apparently broken amidships. Estimated number of

passengers and crew lost, 50; remainder landed and under the care of the German Consul at Harwich." Steerage passengers who were missing were not listed, but among those lost from the first- or second-class cabins were five exiled nuns, whose misspelled names were given as "Barbara Hilkenschmidt, Henrico Tassbander, Lorbela Reenkober, Aurea Radjura, and Brigella Dambard."

Frederick Hopkins, a medical doctor who had entered the Novitiate with Gerard in 1868, and whose suave manner had earned him the nickname of "the genteel Hop," sat on the sofa cushion next to his and glanced at the page. "Are you reading about the *Deutschland*?"

"Very sad, isn't it?"

Thirty-three years later, Frederick would become the Bishop of Honduras, and he would drown in 1923, at age eighty-nine, when the overloaded paddleboat he was on sank in eighteen feet of water. But now the doctor said in his soothing voice, "Well, the sea can be very wild."

Edward Reeve was playing billiards with Cyprian Splaine of Liverpool, a swashbuckling scholastic who was good at whatever game he took on. Reeve tried to distract him by saying, "I can still see our evening menu on your beard, Sib."

Without looking up from his shot, Splaine said, "The front of your cassock displays what we ate *last week*."

There was general laughter, and as Hopkins got up from the sofa, he wryly misquoted Tertullian's praise for Christian love. "Look," Hopkins said, "how they *shove* one another."

Walking to the main chapel, Hopkins heard a sneering wind outside and he thought of it as sea-roaring *Deutschland* weather, carried there as if by the Royal Mail. But in the darkened chapel it was so silent he could hear the faint sweet sibilance as knuckling flames consumed the wicks of the votive candles. He genuflected and sank onto a kneeler six pews back from Christ in the tabernacle and noticed off to his right Brother McKeon saying his Rosary. Reverend William Hayden, an Englishman just three months a priest, was in front of McKeon and tilting toward the ruby glow of the sanctuary light in order to read his breviary.

Casting back on his day in his nightly examination of conscience, Hopkins accused himself of a snorting, sour, unspiritual tone to some of his conversations, prayed for those who'd died, were injured, or lost loved ones in the shipwreck, but thanked God for the beauties and contrarities of nature, the tonic of outdoor exercise, and the cheer and solace of his Jesuit brothers.

•

Thursday it was colder and again snowing, and there were, as usual on Thursdays, no classes, but Hopkins still rose at five-thirty so he could meditate for an hour before the school's seven o'clock Mass.

Sitting with Jerome's Latin Vulgate version of the Bible in his room, Hopkins made the sign of the cross and whispered, "Lord God, grant me the grace that all my intentions, actions, and operations may be directed purely to the service and praise of Thy Divine Majesty." And then he asked for the grace he wanted, which was to surrender his own predilections in order to become a perfect instrument of God's holy will, and to give up whatever was getting in the way of the pleasing sacrifice of Abel: the firstlings of his flock. Reading over the fourth chapter of Genesis, Hopkins agonized that he'd too frequently been like Cain, scrounging fruit fallen onto the ground and presenting that as his lame offering to God and then, justly ignored, and with hurt feelings and envy, slaying a brother with his curt judgments and tart wit. Language his bloody knife. And what were his firstlings? Loyalty, yes, and discipline, education, talent. *These I offer Thee*, Hopkins prayed. But then for the next thirty minutes of meditation there was nothing like a striking insight or a welling up of emotion. Rather than the Scripture passage, his reveries continued hiving around some verses of Milton's *Samson Agonistes*:

Retiring from the popular noise, I seek
This unfrequented place to find some ease,
Ease to the body some, none to the mind
From restless thoughts, that like a deadly swarm
Of Hornets arm'd, no sooner found alone,
But rush upon me thronging, and present
Times past, what once I was, and what am now.

And then he saw it was time for Mass.

•

Cyprian Splaine recruited Hopkins for a *peripatetic*, as he called it, to Denbigh. Splaine was the big, bluff, confident, manly sort that Hopkins found attractive, and Hopkins was vigilant in his vow of chastity, so he obeyed the Rector's rule of "companies" on such hikes—*nunquam duo, semper tres*: never two, always three—a requirement meant to discourage conflicts or particular friendships. Inveigling Billy Splaine, Cyprian's kid brother, to join them, Cyprian advertised Denbigh as a "picturesque town," and Hopkins joked that because of its popularity with tourists Denbigh was even more a "*taking* pictures-esque town."

As they were slogging southward in their black suits and overcoats on a highway now inches deep with snow, Billy gave an excited account of Captain Matthew Webb's heroic suffering during his twenty-two-hour swim of the English Channel, from Dover to Calais, the first to accomplish it, his body slimed with porpoise grease to fend off the murderous cold, his only nourishment cod-liver oil, brandy, beef tea, and strong old ale poured through funnels by friends in dinghies alongside him.

Cyprian smirked. "And now shall we expect you to challenge his speed?"

Billy replied with solemnity, "I'll have to request permission from Father Rector."

Quoting from Shakespeare's *Julius Caesar*, Hopkins recited: "'As he was fortunate, I rejoice at it; as he was valiant, I honour him: but, as he was ambitious, I slew him.'"

Cyprian scowled as he interpreted his friend's meaning and asked, "Are you still studying the Welsh language, Gerard?"

"Rarely," Hopkins said, and then confided to Billy, "I *did* consult Father Rector about it."

"Oh, the Governor's all right."

"Wants us focused on the one holy thing," Cyprian said. "Wants uniformity."

The limekiln under a quarried cliff sent out yellow smoke that dimmed the distance and made the stack of Denbigh Hill a dead, mealy gray, but the sun was sparkling through gaps in the raveled clouds and Hopkins, who noticed architecture, noticed aloud how the castle ruins that crowned the hill were "punched out in bright breaks and eyelets of daylight."

Cyprian was, as always, amused by him. "Sees things," he stage-whispered to his kid brother.

Entrance into the castle required a penny admission charge and they'd scrounged no money from Father Minister, so they instead ate sack lunches by a stone stile under a snowcapped outer wall overgrown with ivy, bramble, and some graceful herb with glossy lush green sprays that were something like celery. Billy had forgotten the Latin for celery, and Cyprian, the finest Hebrew and Latin scholar in the school, took only seconds to answer, *"Apium graveolens,"* and was surprised by their laughter, saying, as Hopkins sat, "Surely a prize student of Jowett knows such things?"

"Jowett?" Billy asked.

Hopkins told him his tutor at Oxford was Reverend Benjamin Jowett, an Anglican theologian who had strayed so near heresy that he largely confined his teaching to Plato and Greek philosophy. Jowett was also an eminent classical scholar who had never visited Athens or Rome. In fact, he seldom left the Oxford campus, staying in touch with those he formerly taught with continual letters of inquiry. "Of him it was written," Hopkins said, " 'First come I. My name is Jowett. There is no knowledge but I know it. I am a tutor in this college. What I don't know isn't knowledge.' "

Billy smiled. "And you're a chip off the old block, aren't you, Hop?"

"Oh, but I have *gaping* holes in my erudition."

And Cyprian told his brother, "You just need to spelunk to find them."

Hiking back to Saint Beuno's, Hopkins taught them some Welsh: *afal* was apple; *aderyn*, bird; *llaeth*, milk; *pysgodyn*, fish. Crow, they knew, was *bran*, for "crow" was Welsh slang for a Jesuit in his black cassock.

And then they saw a vast multitude of starlings making, as Hopkins put it, "an unspeakable jangle." The starlings would settle in a tree, then, stirring and cheering one another, choose another tree in the row to light upon, rising up again at some interior signal. Singularities forgotten. To Hopkins they seemed a cloud of snuff shaken from a wig, many of them in one phase at once, full of zest and delight at hearing each other's cries, all veering black flakes hurling around until they decided in unison to stand quietly in the field. Like his classmates waiting lunch.

"Are they all scholastics, do you think?" Hopkins asked, and Cyprian guffawed.

"Had I a gun, it would rain meat," Billy said.

And his older brother instructed Hopkins, "Remember your steel umbrella when you next visit us in Liverpool."

•

Raisin cakes and Earl Grey tea were served in the gymnasium-sized refectory at five, and then Hopkins went to the scholastics' recreation room to see if *The Times* was available. It was. And he took it with him as he joined a "circle" of Joe Rickaby, Bill Dubberley, and Clement Barraud for an examination review in moral theology. Sydney Smith, an architect and the convert son of an Anglican clergyman, perused his notebook and reminded them, "We have seen that a passion— whether *commotio*, *permotio*, *concitatio*, or *perturbatio*—is nothing other than a movement of the soul caused by the sensate apprehension of a particular good or evil object and accompanied by an organic mutation."

Smith continued with his class notes, but Hopkins instead read the six columns on page 6 that were dedicated to "The Loss of the Deutschland." Readers were reminded that just seven months earlier the *Schiller*, another German transat-

lantic liner, wrecked on the Scilly Isles, southwest of Land's
End, England, and three hundred twelve lives were lost, "a
coincidence of calamities which at present there is no reason for thinking other than fortuitous." The owners of the
Deutschland, the North German Lloyd Company, were their
own insurers, up to now a sound economic decision, for there
had not been a passenger lost at sea in their fleet since the
initial voyage in 1856. The *Liverpool Underwriters' Book of
Iron Vessels* was consulted for the ship's precise length, depth,
width, and tonnage. The writer presumed the captain of the
Deutschland wanted to avoid the shoals of the Dutch coast
with a more westerly course that instead sent the steamship
too close to the shoals of the Thames estuary. There was just
one propeller, and that was lost and unserviceable soon after
the ship struck at five on the morning of December 6th.

When at high tide that night there was flooding in steerage and the upper decks, the passengers were ordered up onto
the masts and spars. "In that cold and terrible night between
Monday and Tuesday," the correspondent wrote, "many unhappy persons must have lost their hold upon the rigging and
fallen numbed into the sea." Quartermaster August Bock's
sail-aided lifeboat washed ashore near the Royal Navy barracks at Sheerness, and he was being skillfully rendered treatment by Staff Surgeon Flanagan, while the cold-blackened
remains of his two boat mates awaited undertaking in the
Duke of Clarence Hotel. A long list of survivors and "missing, presumed dead" was published. It was noted that the
sea-swollen corpse of Adolf Forster, whose ticket number was
52, had just floated ashore at Margate.

There were no photographs, of course, so one's imagina-
tion took over, and Hopkins found himself getting queasy.

But that was all that he had time to skim anyway, for that Thursday night he needed to swot, as they'd said at Oxford, the tiring textbooks for five hour-long lectures the next day, all conducted in Latin. Moral theology was the most technical subject, and Hopkins used up all the coals in his scuttle scrutinizing a treatise on Contracts and memorizing the meanings of *emphyteusis, laudemium, mohatra, antichresis, hypotheca,* and *servitus activa et passiva*—which he would have guessed concerned slavery, but instead concerned easement to properties.

•

His night's sleep was tangled up not by Contracts but by the *Deutschland* reports and the singsong and hammer-and-anvil beats of Longfellow's unjustifiably famous poem "The Wreck of the Hesperus" and its stanzas:

She struck where the white and fleecy waves
   Looked soft as carded wool,
But the cruel rocks, they gored her side
   Like the horns of an angry bull.

Her rattling shrouds, all sheathed in ice,
   With the masts went by the board;
Like a vessel of glass, she stove and sank,
   Ho! Ho! the breakers roared!

Waking on Friday morning with its stupefying awfulness still Ho! Hoing! in his mind, Hopkins was depressed that the stanzas had so deftly found lodging in his memory. "The Wreck of the Hesperus" was the sort of cloying poetry that seagoing tragedies generally inspired in England and America: their sentiments trite, their rhymes forced, their syllabic counts as regular as the ticking of a hallway clock. Whereas he had long had haunting his ear the echo of a new rhythm that would re-create the native and natural stresses of speech.

But the scruples to which he was prey caused Hopkins to consider the worldly pursuit of poetry writing in conflict with his vocation to the priesthood. Just before entering the Society of Jesus in 1868, Hopkins resolved to pen no more verse unless his religious superiors requested it, and in a theatrical act of renunciation he incinerated some copies of his Oxford poems in a secret ceremony that he inconspicuously noted in his journal simply as "the slaughter of the innocents." And that act of renunciation was confirmed for him when, as a novice Jesuit, he was urged to relinquish "disordered attachments" that would impede his freedom and availability for a variety of ministries as well as tempt him to the sin of pride. Since then he'd written only the slightest kinds of poetry: joshing doggerel to entertain at picnics or Latin greeting-card verse for visiting dignitaries.

And yet . . . there was always an interior and hard-to-quell "and yet."

•

His floor swept with sawdust, his clothing on hooks, his gray blankets as taut on his bed as a cavalry sergeant's, Hopkins walked out into a hallway that was wide as a road and wedged his door open in the Jesuit display of owning nothing and having nothing to hide.

Brother Tom Fagan was hurrying down to the kitchen scullery, but winked at him in the Great Silence of Friday's

pre-dawn and yanked his forelock like an earl's footman who
lacked a cap. Smiling and slightly waving a hand in a "Carry
on" gesture, Hopkins headed to the Saint Agnes oratory, and
just for the childishness of it, he skipped down the hallway,
watching the skirt of his cassock flounce.

In the oratory, Hopkins vested himself in a fresh white
surplice with a hem and half-sleeves that were as lacy as the
doilies his mother put under desserts, and then he lit two candles that flanked the tabernacle on the altar, retrieved the
crystal cruets of water and wine from the sacristy, and ribboned the *Missale Romanum* for the Mass of December 10th.

Reverend Bernhard Tepe was late. Waiting for him, Hopkins studied a framed commemorative placard that featured
the photographs of five priests murdered by Communards in
May 1871 after Paris fell in the Franco-Prussian War. The five
had nothing to do with the defeat, but the Church with its
lordly hierarchy and affiliations with the educated elites was
perceived as an anachronism that was resistant to revolution,
and so Pierre Olivaint, Leon Ducoudray, Alexis Clerc, Jean
Caubert, and Anatole de Bengy, all Reverend Fathers of the
Society of Jesus, were executed by gunfire *"en haine de la Foi
catholique,"* in hatred of the Catholic faith.

It was a persecution that the Society of Jesus was now
accustomed to, for in 1868 the Jesuits were expelled from
Spain, and in 1870 the Jesuit curia was expelled from Rome as
the papal states were annexed by King Victor Emmanuel II.
The Jesuit Superior General, Pierre-Jean Beckx, was now
managing the affairs of the Society from Florence. In northern Europe, Chancellor Otto von Bismarck orchestrated the
unification of Prussia, Bavaria, Saxony, Württemberg, and
twenty other states into the Second Reich of Germany, and

originated a *Kulturkampf*, or cultural struggle, that was intended to quash the political power of the country's Catholic minority, which Bismarck loathed for being more loyal to the papacy than to the Reich.

Hopkins was in philosophy studies at Stonyhurst in 1872 when the Reichstag gave the government license to ostracize the Society of Jesus, and the first contingent of exiled German Jesuits arrived in England. And now their Rhineland Theologate was located in Ditton Hall, between Manchester and Liverpool. In May 1873, Culture Minister Adalbert Falk instituted laws giving the Reich control of Catholic education, making civil marriages obligatory and ending all financial aid to the Catholic Church while continuing it for Protestant institutions. And just seven months ago another series of "May Laws" were decreed, excluding from the territories of the Prussian state all Catholic religious orders not involved in the needed job of nursing, and consigning each congregation's properties to the management of a board of trustees selected by the government. Hopkins felt certain the five German nuns who had lost their lives on the *Deutschland* were emigrating from their country because of the Falk Laws.

Reverend Tepe hurried into the oratory, wincing a smile of apology over his tardiness and greeting him with the Latin *"Salve, Frater."*

"Et tu, Pater." And you, Father.

Reverend Bernhard Tepe of Germany was teaching, like Reverend Josef Floeck, dogmatic theology to the newly ordained fourth-year students. Reverend Henrico Legnani oversaw the course of study for those who were not yet priests. And Reverend Emilio Perini of Italy would handle courses in Sacred Scripture at Saint Beuno's for thirteen years. The upheavals on the Continent had contributed the majority of the professors in the British province's only school of theology. Hopkins recalled the curse of Cain: *Thou shalt be a fugitive and vagabond on the earth.*

Reverend Tepe caped his shoulders with a white amice and tied its long strings around his waist. *"Tempestas frigidus,"* he said. Cold weather.

"Ita est," Hopkins said. So it is.

•

The north wind seemed to have teeth as Hopkins used his Friday hour of recreation to scan the snow-covered geography from the heights of the steep hill named Moel y Parch. To the southwest, Mount Snowdon and its children peaks in the range looked like a stack of rugged white flint, streaked with snow, in many places chiseled and channeled. The hedged and stone-fenced farmlands of the vale of Clwyd to the west were the stitched white squares in a shirred quilt that went all the way to the gray ribbon of the Irish Sea and the town of Rhyl, its carnival and silted promenade shut up for the winter. Eastward some twenty miles was Liverpool, its soot and smoke and office buildings no more than gray gorse from that distance. The air smelled cleansed; the leaden sky was roped with cloud; a blue bloom seemed to have spread upon the distant south, enclosed by a basin of hills. And again he felt the charm and instress of Wales.

He turned and saw one black-faced sheep warily staring, as if the seminarian were haunting it, while other sheep dully watched him as they monotonously chewed straw. "Shepherd" in Latin was *pastor*, and he smiled as he thought of himself as twice or thrice pastoral there among the animals, in the graciousness and serenity of a school of theology. Worried at his noticing, the black-faced sheep headed away from him, rousing the others into a hesitant trot, and Hopkins grinned at thinking it another *Kulturkampf* as he went down to Saint Beuno's for classes in canon law and Hebrew.

•

Saturday evening, Rector James Jones strolled into the scholastics' recreation room—an innovation of his governance since the groups of ten ordained professors, seven lay Brothers, and forty-one theologians each had separate dinner tables, housing areas, and recreation rooms in the great three-story mansion, and some considered incursions an insulting act of trespass. But "Father Rector," as he was called, was a manly, rattling, genial, ever-courteous man from County Sligo, Ireland, a shrewd, scientific professor of moral theology who'd studied at the English College in Rome, served as a Superior in British Guiana and Jamaica, and published two scholarly books on the Athanasian creed, yet welcomed contradiction in class and the nickname of "the Governor," delighted in jokes and singing, and so worried about the seminarians' health that he stayed at their bedsides when they were ill, tipping into their mouths his mother's cure-all of hot milk, brandy, and a beaten egg.

Rector Jones joked with the Irish trio of Kelly, Morrogh, and Gavin, and with their laughter left the three and jested in his scratchy Latinity with the scholastics Victor Baudot and Sebastian Sircom, who'd been exiled from France. And then he wandered over to the great fireplace and the half-circle of Irish Georgian wingback chairs where Hopkins was alone with his stare fastened on *The Times*.

"Would it be a discourtesy if I joined you?" the Rector asked.

Hopkins lifted his head and smiled at his fair, tall Superior. "Not at all."

Jones selected the wingback chair next to his. "Don't let me interfere with your reading."

Hopkins held open the newspaper so Jones could see the multiple articles on the *Deutschland* shipwreck. Hopkins told him, "The nuns have been laid out for viewing in the Convent of Jesus and Mary near Stratford. I would guess they'll be interred in Saint Patrick's cemetery, just a mile from where I was born."

The Rector scanned the headlines. "I heard about it, but haven't kept up." Elm logs in the fireplace sang and popped, spewing sparks.

Hopkins read aloud: " 'At two p.m., Captain Brickenstein, knowing that with the rising tide the ship would be waterlogged, ordered all the passengers to come on deck. Danger levels class distinctions, and steerage and first-class passengers were by this time together in the after saloon and cabins. Most of them obeyed the summons at once; others lingered below till it was too late; some of the ill, weak, despairing of life even on deck, resolved to stay in their cabins and meet death without any further struggle to evade it.' "

"Oh dear," Jones said. "Saddening."

Hopkins continued. " 'After three a.m. on Tuesday morning a scene of horror was witnessed. Some passengers clustered for safety within or upon the wheelhouse, and on the top of other slight structures on deck. Most of the crew and many of the emigrants went into the rigging, where they were safe enough as long as they could maintain their hold. But the intense cold and long exposure told a tale.' "

"Cold wind, icy seas," said Jones. "Horrible in combination."

" 'The purser of the ship, though a strong man, relaxed his grasp, and fell into the sea. Women and children and men were one by one swept away from their shelters on the deck.' And here it's quite moving, Father: 'Five German nuns, whose bodies are now in the dead-house here, clasped hands and were drowned together, the chief sister, a gaunt woman six feet high, calling out loud and often "O Christ, come quickly!" till the end came. The shrieks and sobbing of women and children are described by the survivors as agonizing.' "

Jones sighed, *"Requiescant in pace,"* but then glanced over at his underling. Hopkins was so greatly affected by the account that he was close to tears.

Jones kindly considered him and said, "Perhaps someone should write a poem on the subject." And then the Rector gently patted Hopkins's forearm and got up to heartily greet some theologians who'd just entered.

Hopkins touched a handkerchief to each eye and left *The Times* for others on a gleaming library table as he walked out. Although he'd at first intended to visit the main chapel for his nightly prayers in the presence of the Blessed Sacrament, his thoughts were racing, and in the rapture of inspiration he hurried up the stairs to his room in "The Mansions." And though his "hand was out at first," as he later admitted, Hopkins managed by midnight to pen eight lines:

> On Saturday sailed from Bremen,
>> American-outward-bound,
>>> Take settler and seaman, tell men with women,
>>>> Two hundred souls in the round—

O Father, not under thy feathers nor ever as guessing
  The goal was a shoal, of a fourth the doom to be drowned;
    Yet did the dark side of the bay of thy blessing
Not vault them, the millions of rounds of thy mercy not reeve even
  them in?

2

THE EMIGRANTS
FROM SALZKOTTEN

The five were Sister Barbara Hültenschmidt, aged thirty-two; Sister Norberta Reinkober, thirty; Sister Henrica Fassbender, twenty-eight; Sister Brigitta Dammhorst, twenty-seven; and Sister Aurea Badziura, twenty-three—all of a religious congregation called the Sisters of Saint Francis, Daughters of the Sacred Hearts of Jesus and Mary, founded by Mother Clara Pfänder in 1859.

On Thursday, December 2nd, 1875, just before the Offertory at a sunrise Mass in their convent in Salzkotten, Germany, each of them singly knelt in front of Mother Clara, their eyes silvering with tears of bliss and their hands in prayer. Each wore a black veil that fell to the waist and was indented at its peak like a valentine heart, with a starched white headband and hair-and-neck-hiding wimple; their habits chocolate-brown wool with a white cord cincture and a five-decade rosary hanging along their left thighs. With Mother Clara's soft hands gently shut over theirs, each professed the handwritten vows of poverty, chastity, and obedience that each would fold into leather phylacteries and hide underneath their habits like necklace amulets. She gave each a platinum gold wedding ring to wear as symbol of her marriage to Christ.

The foundress had already spoken on the vows. Owning nothing, she'd said, they were joining the poorest of the poor in accepting their dependence on God. In chastely forsaking the intimate love of all others, they were freely offering their hearts and bodies in a holy pledge to the One who loved them into being. Obedience was an invitation to faithfulness to their Superior, their community, and the constitutions of the congregation, accepting the hardships of their vows as continuing channels of grace. The five were also promising to be available to every need of the poor in America, especially in hospitals and orphanages, "to aid by zealous prayer our holy Catholic Church" and "to integrate the contemplative and active life so that the latter is nourished, strengthened, and supported through the former, and thus becomes itself rich in blessings."

After Mass there was a feast in the refectory: instead of just pumpernickel bread and weak coffee, there were waffles, sour cherries, a honey and apple purée, soft smoked sausages, and Oldenburg tea. Quiet conversation at breakfast was permitted for the instant, and the foundress even overlooked some uncommon disorder as the hundred nuns still in the motherhouse went from one to another of the five, holding their hands as they offered continuing prayers or hugging them in farewell. Many wept. "Little birds must fly," Sister Aurea squeakily said of herself, and she was indulged, as always, with laughter.

There was an ovation when the five Sisters stood for one last time at Salzkotten's refectory doors, waving jubilantly and smiling as if they were off on a wilderness expedition, and then the foundress escorted them out to the public entrance of the huge, three-story convent where ten of the older orphan boys whom they'd schooled and nursed and mothered were waiting beside their five identical black portmanteaus, each identified with their family names in Sister Brigitta's gold, Teutonic calligraphy.

While the five got into their black woolen cloaks and knitted gloves, the orphans teamed at carrying the trunks out to a four-horse landau and scrabbled up to the carriage's roof to receive the trunks as others handed them up. Some boys displaced their feelings of abandonment and sorrow by shouting insolence and contradiction at each other. And then like footmen they bowed from the waist as the five nuns modestly strolled out, touched the heads or cheeks of the boys in goodbye, and got into the carriage, three facing two so the full length of tall Sister Barbara's legs would be at liberty. Mother Clara gave the coachman marks from a purse, and the carriage tilted as the heavy man climbed up to his seat, and then the foundress stood afar from them, suppressing any hint of loss as she waved to five daughters she feared she might never see again, so far away, in Missouri. The horses jerked the carriage forward, and Sister Norberta and Sister Aurea hung out the open windows for a final glimpse of Mother Clara hunching forward into the convent to join the nuns in the motherhouse for adoration of the Blessed Sacrament, praying that Christ in the tabernacle and in the world would shelter and keep the emigrants on their long voyage west.

Sister Aurea first, and then Sister Norberta, found it exceedingly cold in the hawkish wind, and they soon dropped back inside the coach, moonily gazing at the dear-to-their-hearts motherhouse until, at a highway turning, interfering elm trees leapt in the way. Sister Norberta whimpered.

"Don't be like Lot's wife," Sister Brigitta said.

Sister Norberta frowned in confusion.

"She looked over her shoulder with regret and was turned into a pillar of salt."

Sister Norberta crossly instructed Sister Brigitta, "But that was Sodom and Gomorrah. And those cities were destroyed because of their wickedness."

Sister Brigitta looked away, holding her tongue.

"Our convent's not like that," Sister Norberta insisted. "It's a holy place."

"She's just saying we have glorious opportunities to look forward to," Sister Barbara said.

"But I'm not like Lot's wife," said Sister Norberta.

"And don't speak for me," Sister Brigitta told Sister Barbara. "I have words. I can explain myself perfectly well."

Sister Barbara folded her arms like a forbearing husband.

With calm, Sister Henrica said, "We're all feeling emotional right now."

Sister Brigitta's mouth was quivering. "Sister Norberta's the temperamental one."

"Don't you 'don't' me," Sister Norberta commanded.

Sister Henrica fashioned a smile, but her tone was firm. "Shall we be silent, please?"

Silence flooded the coach.

•

Sister Henrica was born Catharina Fassbender in the Imperial City of Aachen on April 19th, 1847. Her father, Wilhelm, was a hearty, tireless, and adored eighth-grade teacher in the School of the Holy Cross. Since Wilhelm's wife had also been baptized Catharina, they nicknamed their firstborn Nettchen, and she was called by that diminutive even into her teens. She was the oldest of seven children. Teachers thought her good or satisfactory in the classes she took in grammar school, though her handwriting and needlework were considered poor and she was often sleepily late for class. Because Aachen was just across the border from Belgium, she learned the French language at the School of the Holy Cross, and after graduation attended the Institute of Saint Leonard, which was run by Ursuline nuns. There she studied English, earning the highest grade in the class.

Catharina was just fifteen when her mother died in child-birth, and the girl was forced to take on the jobs of feeding and clothing her sisters and brothers and sternly supervising their household chores. Until the funeral, Catharina had not been conspicuously pious, but afterward she developed a hunger for prayer, and she received twenty-two holy cards from the Ursulines as prizes for her exams in religion and Bible history and for her conscientiousness in attending daily Mass. She graduated from the institute at Easter, at the age of sixteen, and first took a job in a shop selling baby clothes and then in a printing establishment run by the Scholl sisters. The Scholl sisters would write of Catharina Fassbender, "She conducted herself in an exemplary manner in our shop, so that we can now recommend her with the utmost confidence."

She was pretty and petite, a sprite, only five foot two in height, with a child's soft voice, sorrel-brown hair woven into an intricate bun, flashing, witty, sky-blue eyes, and the healthy body of a skilled gymnast. In a hundred years no less than two of Catharina Fassbender's relatives would become international opera stars, and the harbinger of that singing talent was heard in her lovely contralto. She still lived at home so she could help with the children, but her father worried that her work and child-care hours were too long and hard and joyless, and he had begun seeing a music teacher whom Catharina seemed to consider a rival, so Wilhelm Fassbender hired an old Belgian woman to serve as his housekeeper and sent his oldest daughter fifty miles northeast to Cologne to clerk in the fashionable dress shop of a former classmate's widow, a haughty woman named Frau Kettgen.

Each morning Catharina attended a six-thirty Mass in the glorious Cologne Cathedral, faithfully praying for her mother and the other poor souls in Purgatory, then walked to work turning the pages of volumes by Friedrich Klopstock or Christoph Wieland or a shocking naturalist novel by Émile Zola that she would later mention in Confession. She stocked shelves with skirts, jerseys, and fancy stockings, handled financial transactions, filled out orders in French and English for the fall line of clothing from wholesalers in Paris and London. Then she'd idly wander home to her attic room, head down in a book that she held like a hymnal.

Renting a room below her was a hugely overweight jeweler with a very large brain who invited her down for schnitzel and sauerkraut and weekly monologues on the philosophy of Leibniz, Hegel, and Kant. There were also gentlemen who escorted her to the Cologne symphony or a thunderous opera by Richard Wagner, or on easy Sunday strolls along the Rhine, but Catharina did not mention a name more than twice, and her employer felt it would be too Italian to pry. Widow Kettgen considered the girl efficient, fastidious, honest, intelligent, and practical, if slightly otherworldly in her bookishness. She would write formally to Mother Clara: "In spite of her young years, I have always been able to leave the shop in Fräulein Fassbender's care."

Widow Kettgen wrote Mother Clara, as the Scholl sisters had, because Catharina Fassbender affected an interest in joining the Salzkotten religious order after Sister Benedicta Eickhoff and Sister Philomena Oldegeering entered the Cologne dress shop to beg alms from the customers, the owner, and the clerk. Sister Benedicta explained that they were from a newly established convent near Paderborn, and since they ran a school and orphanage for the neediest children, their only income was in the form of gracious donations from outsiders. Catharina noticed that indeed their skeletal hands and faces were those of the famished, and there otherwise seemed to be no scheming or false pretense in them. She felt their clear, serene, and shining eyes peering so deeply into hers it was like an injection, and they seemed to find something interesting in the shopgirl that she herself had not. Even after they had received a goodly sum of money from Catharina and Frau Kettgen and some customers, the Sisters tarried in the dress shop for an hour, answering the shopgirl's many questions about the congregation and its goals and stoical way of living, and Sister Benedicta printed out the Salzkotten mailing address on a form meant for tailor measurements.

Catharina felt exalted and mysteriously altered by the chance meeting, and when, three weeks later, she received materials on the Salzkotten convent, she read again and again Mother Clara's intentions concerning the education of orphans:

> The Sisters impart a complete elementary education to all children admitted to their home, train the girls in needlework, and give them practice in the performance of domestic duties. Their charges may not be dismissed until they have received

sufficient elementary education, made their first Holy Communion, and are in a position to earn their own livelihood. When the Sisters release their charges, they endeavor to procure for them an occupation which will be favorable to the children's moral welfare in the world. They keep them in mind as their own children and support them at all times with counsel and help.

She felt thrilled by that in ways she could not quite explain to Widow Kettgen, except to say that all her talents, experience, and hidden desires seemed to be enunciated in that one paragraph.

And so when she visited the Salzkotten convent, she was giddy with excitement. Mother Clara was not yet forty-five, but she was confident, shrewd, sovereign, and missed nothing, and she silently and tactlessly scrutinized the shopgirl as Catharina sat on a green chenille sofa in the office of the foundress and said she'd never been so certain of the rightness of anything as she was about religious life. Suddenly so much seemed irrelevant. Suddenly everything in her history made sense. "I feel," she said, "I finally have let go of heavy weights and found out I can float."

"Well put," the foundress said. She recalled just that feeling. She was Anna Theresia Pfänder, the wealthy and overwooed daughter of the mayor of Hallenberg, when she herself sought instead of marriage entrance into the congregation of the Sisters of Christian Charity. She would leave them after nine years, not out of spite or dissatisfaction, but to found another, poorer religious order. She quoted the Gospel of Matthew, in which Jesus spoke of his yoke being easy and his burden light, noting, "When our vocation is from God, no matter how difficult it may otherwise seem, it is not a burden. We feel light." She startled Catharina by admitting that she too had lost her mother and then her stepmother to illnesses as a girl, and when the Mayor, as she called her father, married yet a third time, six more children were added to the earlier eight and it fell to Anna to mother them all. She now felt certain that Christ was simply preparing her for the job of establishing this congregation of holy and sometimes trying women.

"Surely, that's true," Catharina said. "I feel Jesus has prepared me in just the same way."

The face of the foundress clouded. "Oh? Would you like to be me?"

The girl flushed and shifted uneasily on the sofa.

Mother Clara smiled. "Don't worry, dear. I find being me *exceedingly* attractive."

Catharina giggled like a child on a swing, and as she continued in conversation with the foundress, she felt they'd been friends for years; in fact, she felt increasingly that she was speaking to the mother she'd lost at age fifteen, that she was being called to join this convent from Heaven. With embarrassment she confessed that, and Mother Clara just smiled and said she was used to hearing those feelings expressed, not generally from aspirants, but within the first year or two of their entrance, as healthy females hot with love sought a safe object of affection.

And then Mother Clara cautiously said, "Everything I have read about your character and heard from you now is quite satisfactory." She stood. "Will you please visit your father and family for a while and try to join us March eighteenth?"

And so it was that in 1871, three weeks before she turned twenty-four, Catharina Fassbender went to Salzkotten and became a postulant in the motherhouse of the Sisters of Saint Francis, Daughters of the Sacred Hearts of Jesus and Mary. On September 24th of that year she received the habit and the name Sister Mary Henrica, after Mary, the mother of Jesus, and Heinrich, the eleventh-century Emperor of Bavaria who became a saint.

Sister Benedicta said of her that she took to the convent like a kitten to cream, and she gradually became, like her father the schoolteacher, zealous, hardworking, and much adored, a friendly, sympathetic, and nimble-witted young woman who was held up to the newest postulants as a model of wisdom, prudence, and piety. She was devoted to Mother Clara, and Mother Clara to her, and if it was no surprise to others that Sister Henrica was chosen, at age twenty-eight, to head the American foundation of the order, it was a great sacrifice and loss for the foundress, who realized that only selfish affection constrained her from making such an obvious choice.

She had called Sister Henrica out of a nursery as she secretly taught the children how to pray—the sort of religious instruction that Otto von Bismarck and the Falk Laws no longer allowed. Sister Henrica thought she'd been called into the hallway to be scolded for that illegal initiative, and was about to apologize when Mother Clara quietly and quickly told the schoolteacher that she would be going to Missouri, near the city of Saint Louis, as a hospital nurse and the religious Superior of the American province of their congregation.

The younger nun had been teaching the "Angelus." She took in what she'd heard, and after a silence repeated a line from that prayer in which the Virgin Mary says at the Annunciation, "Be it done unto me according to thy word."

And too soon it was December 2nd, and the five were riding north in a landau, and Mother Clara walked into her office in the motherhouse from the hour of adoration, finding on the floor a handwritten poem in Shakespearean blank verse of five accented syllables per line. She stayed standing as she read:

FAREWELL

Now the solemn hour of departure is at hand,
And my heart, deeply touched, throbs with fear;
'Tis bleeding as though pierced by many a spear,
For in bitter pain we leave you and our land so dear.

I leave—yes, depart gladly and in peace—
In obedience to your wishes, O Mother most dear;
Though distant, I know that your prayers will ne'er cease,
For your love will follow—hov'ring ever near.

There were stanzas in which Sister Henrica mentioned "a torn heart," "hot tears," and "many a sigh," but she wrote that she would be consoled by Mother Clara's prayers and blessings, and she realized:

I need not fear—God knows best my every need—
Is he not ruler over land and sea?

For me beg the courage, the strength, and the power
That holy zeal for his honor within me may burn;
That humbly his glory I increase in each hour,
While striving his Holy Will to perform.

Mother Clara skipped to the final three stanzas and read:

Farewell! Hallowed Spot, where so oft I have knelt
Farewell! Our Convent Chapel, so dear!
For here in thy sanctuary oft have I felt
God's plea: "Draw nigh to me here!"

Farewell! Holy Statues—perhaps forever!
You who so peacefully down on me gaze,
As though you'd say: "You too must endeavor
Your eyes to Heaven always to raise."

Farewell! Farewell! You Hallowed Rooms—
Where I have lived so happily without pain;
Farewell! You Gardens and all you lovely trees—
Farewell! Farewell! and *Auf Wiedersehen*!

Dedicated to our dearly beloved Venerable Mother
at our departure for America
by
Your loving daughter, grateful unto death,
Sister M. Henrica
Salzkotten, December 2, 1875

Mother Clara carried the poem to her office desk, slid it into a folder, and held her face in her hands as she tried not to cry. She was unsuccessful for a while, and then, sighing, she got the mail she'd sought and went outside to greet the postman.

•

The five Sisters stayed in a Hannover hotel Thursday night, found a six o'clock Mass on Friday morning, and were at the railway station by eight a.m. Cold winds from the north caused them to cringe together on the platform for the train heading north toward Bremen. Some passengers who'd joined the Chancellor's culture struggle sought to demonstrate their enlistment by widely avoiding the Sisters or sneering with deliberate rudeness, but the five religious hardly noticed as they whisperingly prayed the sorrowful mysteries of the Rosary.

When that was concluded with a sign of the cross, Sister Aurea asked, "Mother Henrica? Could we each have some pfennigs for hot coffee?"

She was told, "Call me *Sister*, please, until we cross the Atlantic." Sister Henrica peeked into her coin purse at a great wealth of folded marks that were meant to last five women three weeks. She did the mathematics. "And no," she said. "We shall fast until we reach the port of Bremerhaven."

Sister Aurea sulked until the northbound train arrived, and then she rushed childishly onto it as a sighing Sister Barbara hauled up her portmanteau.

Sister Henrica watched the four find facing seats together as the train jerked forward; then she got into a lone window seat behind them on the screeching, shifting railway car, scanning a Rhine Valley countryside that was plotted and pieced with farms. There were fields of shorn barley or wheat, now blond and fallowed with winter, Jersey cattle sedately chewing silage in their pens, their hides ruffed like hackles in the cold, sodden, pillowy gray quilts of cloud hanging so close they seemed just out of reach of her hand. The railroad was channeled alongside a green, slow, weed-skirted Weser River that was wide enough for oceangoing vessels but was now silting up so high that even fishing boats sometimes ran aground and the southern port at Bremen could no longer be used. Off in the eastern distance, hurdles of leafless trees ducked and eddied with the wind, and soon, just above their writhing, the many spires and towers and chimneyed, slate-roofed buildings of a city inched up. She heard Sister Norberta and Sister Brigitta in disputation over which city it was, and she smiled in a motherly way as she fell asleep.

•

The five Sisters got to their hotel at the port of Bremerhaven in the late afternoon, and Sister Aurea was given permission to stroll outside if she could get another Sister to join her. She chose Sister Brigitta.

Sister Aurea and Sister Brigitta first walked to the Lloyd's Hall, where, high overhead, easterly breezes were snapping the colorful flags from international ports of call. The gray, shingled sky was glooming with nightfall and the seaside temperature of twenty-nine degrees felt far colder than that in the veil-snatching wind. But inside the hall were grand, heated waiting rooms with green velvet chairs and sculpted benches and ornate gardens of tropical trees and flowers painted on their walls and high ceilings, where hundreds of travelers leaving Germany huddled with their luggage and the heirloom possessions they would carry to the New World and hand down to their children's children. Sister Henrica had handed Sister Brigitta just enough pfennigs to treat themselves to cups of hot Russian chocolate milk in the restaurant, and on their way out, Sister Aurea inquired about the ship named *Deutschland* that was bound for New York City. She was surprised to hear it already was anchored at the port, on

the eastern quay of the Weser River. She hurried outside to
see it in its mooring, and Sister Brigitta got a brochure for the
vessel at a grilled ticket window.

Strolling under the wakening gaslights, Sister Brigitta
read that the steamship *Deutschland* was constructed at the
Caird Yard at Greenock in Scotland, and was launched on
May 30th, 1866. The steamship was just one of twenty-nine
vessels in the fleet of the North German Lloyd line—ranked
first among the world's shipping companies, with more than
forty thousand passengers per year—and Sister Brigitta was
pleased to note that since they had commenced operations
in 1857 not one of the Lloyd fleet's passengers was ever lost
at sea.

She'd caught up to Sister Aurea, who called, "See how
huge it is, Sister Brigitta! Huge as a cathedral!"

Sister Brigitta looked at an iron hull that was newly
painted in a shining black enamel she thought too funereal,
and then high overhead at midship she saw a giant black funnel that had been freshly cleaned of its coal soot. There was a
four-story-high foremast with a sail that was partly loose and
luffing in the cold wind of twilight, and aft of the funnel were
spiderwebs of rope on a far taller mainmast that held the under sail, the topsail, the topgallant sail, and the royal sail of
what she would learn was called brigantine rigging. Along its
sheer line were perhaps forty portholes for what she presumed were the first- and second-class cabins. She glanced at
the brochure again and told Sister Aurea the *Deutschland*
had five bulkheads, whatever those were, and was three hundred twenty feet long, thirty-eight feet deep, and forty-two
feet in width. "Width," she said, "is called beam, for some
reason."

"And lifeboats?"

"Eight," Sister Brigitta read. "Seven are iron and one is wooden. Each can accommodate seventy people."

"And how many shall we be?"

Sister Brigitta shrugged. "They say it's equipped for eighty in first class, one hundred twenty in second class, and six hundred in steerage."

They strolled forward on a wide pier of tarred wood, water sloshing and smacking against the pilings underneath them as overhead a flock of seagulls soared and swooped and loudly hunted food before nightfall became final. The gear and tackle and trim of a transatlantic steamship and its seamen were piled high on the dock and a half-dozen dockhands were hauling cases of food and wine up a gangplank. Sister Aurea was still frowning over the arithmetic. She finally said, "So they'd be short. Eight hundred passengers, and the lifeboats can hold only five hundred sixty."

"Emigration is slackening now. We'll have possibly one or two hundred only. And there are a thousand cork life vests, too."

"Are you afraid?" Sister Aurea asked.

Looking north, Sister Brigitta could just make out the flashing light tower that marked the harbor's entrance. "Don't be silly," Sister Brigitta said.

She sensed she was being stared at and discovered high above her two older dock workers hanging over the gunwale of the aft deck, muttering about the nuns in secret tones and unmistakably leering. "Aren't you pretty!" one yelled.

She immediately turned and scuttled toward the Lloyd's Hall with her head down, and when Sister Aurea caught up to her, Sister Brigitta said, "I was fibbing. I'm afraid."

•

She was born October 15th, 1848, and christened Maria Elisabeth, but was called Lisette. Her mother and father were *Kötters*, tenant farmers, on the plains of Mastholte, now Rietberg, twenty-five miles north of Salzkotten.

With children her own age Lisette was pettish, sensitive, and timid. Whereas with her older brothers she put on such princess airs that she was teased until she played the martyr and fell in a faint to the floor. She was ill so often at age ten that Mastholte's doctor told her mother to have Lisette lie on a seaweed mattress, but Frau Dammhorst soon found underneath the seaweed Dutch elm branches that her strange, pretty daughter had put there to disturb her sleep so she could "ease the pain of the souls in Purgatory." The girl fasted once a week, gave up meat and eggs at age twelve, got the highest grades in whatever art or religion class she was in, and was given to theatrical pieties such as "Oh, Mother, I felt the nicest interior joy as I made my novena this afternoon," or "I shall have to keep close guard of my senses lest I fall again into sin." Her Christian faith was authentic, but she knew only how to talk in the catechetical language of others. The most difficult question anyone could ask Lisette was "How do you feel?"

She attended a *Volksschule* where she did well in the dreary subjects of childhood and also learned to paint in watercolors and play the clavichord and zither. Then she was sent away to a Catholic boarding school for girls that stressed culinary skills, etiquette, and good housekeeping in addition to the liberal arts, music, and religion. There she hung above her trundle bed a purple needlepoint of her motto: "Walk in love. Ephesians 5:2." She kept a journal and wrote in it at age sixteen: "Called to convent." But the Dammhorst finances were such that upon graduation she was forced to find work wherever she could, and after three years of humble placements she took a job as a maid in the household of the lawyer and notary Wilhelm Tiltmann in Lippstadt, west of Salzkotten. She found him wise and courtly and overly fond of her, his friendly gaze lingering on her face and figure and forlornly changing as she left his rooms, his hands straying against hers as she served him food, then hastily withdrawing. In his letter of recommendation to Mother Clara and the Sisters of Saint Francis, Herr Tiltmann "gladly" confided that Lisette "not only faithfully fulfilled her obligations and gave no cause for complaint, but was excellent also in her demureness, diligence, and good behavior."

She was a lithe, beautiful, unsmiling blonde with stunning eyes that were blue as Dresden ware, and with shy ways that could seem haughty. She was vain about her hands and nails, but she worried over slight flaws in her face, was vexed by a half-twist in a front tooth, and chagrined by breasts she thought as large as globes. She inspired hankering and heartache in men, and even older women adoringly watched as she strolled gracefully down the street. And she hated the attention, hated the stupidity of desire, hated the worldliness she felt whenever she dragged an ivory brush through her gorgeous, platinum, raveling hair.

She was in a Lippstadt church just before Mass when a phalanx of school nuns quietly entered the front two pews on the left side and knelt in silent unison. The first thought Lisette had was how hidden they were in their habits and veils, and then how loved by Love she would feel were she to give everything up to his service and prayer. When in the summer she wrote her parents that she still felt "a haunting attraction to religious life in an order with rigorous discipline," her mother angrily wrote back a three-page letter nagging that Lisette had been headstrong since childhood, took religion too seriously, had not the slightest idea of the privations of convent life, was cruelly wringing her mother's heart, and hadn't "given marriage a chance." And her father insisted in a postscript printed with a flat carpenter's pencil whose point he'd no doubt wet with his tongue, "You can have *anyone!*"

Reading that, she at once agreed with him: she *could* have anyone for a bridegroom. And she'd chosen Jesus.

To please her parents she went to a September party near their Mastholte farm in a fine silver gown made of silk and damask, but she was so ill at ease with the lovelorn intensity of a veterinarian who considered himself her primary suitor that she was found hiding in an attic, reading Schiller, when her father fetched her at eleven. Riding home with him in his surrey that night, she thought he was fuming for want of an apology, but before she could form one, Herr Dammhorst concluded his ruminations by saying, "I'll take you to see the pastor on Wednesday. But please, no convent with strict enclosure. Your mother and I want to see you."

And so it was that Herr Dammhorst was sulking behind Lisette, and using a stick to scrape mud from his boots into a wastepaper basket, when she informed the pastor she hoped to join the Congregation of the Franciscan Sisters in Salzkotten.

Wiping the stick off on his trousers, the *Kötter* interrupted to ask, "What do *they* do?"

The pastor mildly told him, "Mother orphans, nurse the sick, educate children."

Her father gruffly said, "She's shy. She'll hate teaching."

Lisette was stern when she faced him. "But I wouldn't hate it there."

The pastor escorted the applicant to his secretary's desk in the hall in order to have her fill out some paperwork, and while she was away he asked Herr Dammhorst, "Tell me: What is the worst quality in your daughter?"

Without hesitation he answered, "She's sanctimonious."

The pastor smiled. "She'll lose that in the convent."

On October 1st, 1871, the Lippstadt pastor wrote a subdued letter of recommendation for her entrance into Mother Clara's congregation, noting that "Miss Elisabeth Dammhorst from Mastholte, who has lived here for eighteen months, has conducted herself well and to the satisfaction of her employer at whose home she resided during the time that she has been here."

She entered Salzkotten November 30th, 1871. A year later, on November 7th, 1872, she received the habit and the name Brigitta, after the canonized Queen of Sweden. Three mornings a week she taught art or music to the orphans; otherwise she organized the piano recitals and the singing club, called a *Liederkranz*; alternated with another Sister in playing organ in the chapel; was the calligrapher of the many labels, signs, rules, and announcements in the motherhouse; and helped the nurse in the children's infirmary, sticking mustard plasters on their chests as a counterirritant, spooning castor oil into their unhappy mouths, heating their cold bedsheets in winter with a hot iron, and solemnly warning the boys who'd fallen in love with her and were faking their illness, "You must get well very soon or you shall have to sleep on seaweed."

On May 24th, 1875, Sister Brigitta consecrated her life to the worship and service of God through temporary vows. Just one week later there was a congregation meeting at which a concerned Mother Clara read aloud a public notice by Count Otto von Bismarck and his government decreeing: "All religious orders and similar groups are to be excluded from the territories of the Prussian state. New foundations are prohibited; those already existing are to be disbanded within six months; for foundations whose members serve to instruct and educate youth, the period of grace may be extended up to four years by the Minister of Culture, if no substitutes can be found." But the foundress noted that the announcement also stated: "Establishments of religious orders or similar groups who devote themselves exclusively to the care of the sick may continue; they may, however, be dissolved by the decree of the monarchy. The continuing existence of religious orders and similar groups is dependent on the opinion of the government."

Mother Clara told the assembled Sisters that Bismarck once complained of insomnia by saying, "I have spent the whole night hating." And he chiefly loathed Catholicism, which he considered the religion of Italians and peasants. While Bismarck was in power, she warned, the opinion of the government would never again be gracious to their Church. "We shall not flee persecution," she said. "Christians never have. But I shall welcome opportunities elsewhere if we can be of greater use."

Immediately after that meeting, Sister Brigitta was told she would become a surgical assistant to Salzkotten's Dr. Damm so she could improve her nursing skills—the first hint she had that she soon might be sent to join the nineteen other

Salzkotten Sisters who were now nurses in the newly constructed Saint Boniface Hospital in Carondelet. She studied a
map and found Carondelet south of Saint Louis in the state of
Missouri in the country that Sister Brigitta knew only as *die
Vereinigten Staaten von Amerika.*

She began to study English.

•

Since Friday, December 3rd, would be their last night in Germany, Sister Henrica reserved seating for five at the first-class
Wiegelmann restaurant, where they splurged on shared appe-
tizers of oysters, mussels, and lobster soup, then entrees of
Rügen eels with golden brown bellies, fillets of plaice served
with curly kale, Matjes herring and potatoes, and then
desserts of sweet marzipan from Lübeck and heated snifters
of caraway brandy. Soon they were jolly and Sister Aurea was
telling slightly risqué jokes she'd learned from an uncle, and
Sister Norberta tilted close to Sister Henrica to confide,
"They're all staring at us."

Sister Henrica looked around at censorious wives with
gloved hands and jewels, and scowling husbands with stiff
spines and stiff white collars, some with cheeks scarred by
fencing swords. She smiled as she told Sister Norberta, "I
don't really care."

Also dining there that night and heeding the nuns as he
ate sauerbraten alone was Eduard Brickenstein, who had just
been promoted from his job as master, or captain, of the
steamship *Rhine* for the loftier command of the *Deutschland*,
which he considered the luxurious *grande dame* of the North
German Lloyd ocean liners. Brickenstein was forty-five, a
sturdy, square-chested Lutheran whose father had been the

director of the Institute for the Education and Instruction of Young Gentlemen in the village of Rantzau in Schleswig-Holstein—the highly contested duchies of Denmark that Prussia had annexed just a decade earlier. He spoke four languages, including a fluent English, and had been told by many American passengers over the years that he seemed a younger, handsomer version of President Ulysses S. Grant, whom he supposed he did resemble with his hawkish, shrewd eyes, his groomed, graying beard, and the fussily brushed, sable-brown hair that was ever so gradually receding from his forehead.

Eduard Brickenstein grew up near the Baltic Sea, fished from dories there as a boy, got his start as a seaman on a three-masted sailing ship while still a teenager, and swiftly rose to first mate, then first officer, and on his first try succeeded in the exacting tests for "Master of Vessels." Certified as a "Ship's Navigator" by both the German and American governments, he had a conscientious, serious, scientific mind, and he possessed such enormous stamina that one first mate swore Brickenstein never slept and a friend called him "as constant and industrious as a piston." Sixteen years now he'd been a ship's master, eight of them with North German Lloyd, and he'd conducted over a hundred voyages from the harbor of Bremerhaven to the British port of call in Southampton Water, and then across the North Atlantic to the final destination of New York City. And he'd never lost a life. A Bremen newspaper would write of Captain Brickenstein: "It would be hard to find a man with a greater sense of duty, self-sacrifice, caution, and presence of mind than he, and the confidence of his superiors speak for his sound professional knowledge. At the same time he has always been concerned for the comfort of his passengers, and has sought, as a good host, to make their stay as comfortable as possible."

Watching the five exiled nuns getting into their cloaks to exit the restaurant, he finished off his dinner with a liqueur glass of Steinhäger schnapps and was standing up from his table and neatening his black bow tie and black, double-breasted captain's suitcoat in an oval wall mirror when August Bock, one of his quartermasters, hurried inside the restaurant, jostling the headwaiter.

Brickenstein walked over to him and made an old and obvious joke about the ramming, for *Bock*, in German, means "he-goat." And the quartermaster apologized for his lateness, claiming his little girls were wailing and clinging to his trouser legs and wouldn't let him go.

"Are they always that way?" the captain asked.

"My wife got them worried. She believes we are going to have an unlucky time of it."

Brickenstein fired a flinty look at him.

"Wives," August Bock sheepishly said. "Worrying always."

"Well, you missed a fine meal," the captain said. "Shall we see our ship?"

August Bock was raised in Bremerhaven, and seafaring was the only life he'd ever fantasized about as a child. Hiring on with North German Lloyd at the height of the emigration to America, he'd advanced in rank until he was forced to serve as a naval chief petty officer in the ten-month Franco-Prussian War that effected the unification of northern and southern Germany. Then he rejoined the Lloyd company as a quartermaster in charge of fuel and signal flares and navigating instruments. August Bock was now thirty and a fit six foot two, a handsome man whose shaved face was scarlet with windburn and whose shock of blond hair was still cut close to the sides of his head in the Navy style. Emigration was now slackening, and of Lloyd's fleet of twenty-five transatlantic ships only seven were still making the crossing. Bock feared he would soon receive the redundancy notice that had laid off so many other officers and crew, but he'd managed to learn a little English, which made him seem more functional than those limited to their mother tongue.

Waiting for the quartermaster and the captain on the weather deck of the S.S. *Deutschland* was August Lauenstein, the scarecrow first officer. Cold, howling winds scented with snow were tilting the skinny old man off-balance as he held a coal-oil lamp high overhead and saluted as the officers climbed the gangway. Shouting his welcome, Lauenstein tightened his peacoat collar at his neck and nodded his head toward the pilothouse. "Shall we get out of this?"

Workers sidestepped by them with crates. A harried population was developing on the main deck. Captain Brickenstein silently walked aft, and First Officer Lauenstein shifted places with the quartermaster, who fell in behind them.

August Bock had reported that the ship would not be deeply laden, for she would be hauling a cargo of general merchandise in the amount, or burthen, of only fourteen hundred tons, though she was registered to hold nearly two thousand. And now August Lauenstein informed the captain that there would be only one hundred thirteen passengers.

"Crew?" Brickenstein loudly asked.

"Ninety-nine," Lauenstein shouted, and retrieved from an inside pocket of his black peacoat three folded sheets of paper with handwriting in the florid penmanship of the day. "I have the list," he said.

Brickenstein took it from him as he entered the pilot-house at the ship's stern. It was the size of a Victorian parlor, overheated with steam radiators and lighted by gas jet hurricane lamps that hung from sconces on the freshly painted white walls. Wind was snoring through chinks and flaws in its eight plate-glass windows. The helm was locked in place with rope halters, and just in front of it inside a round brass casing was a compass that was as wide as a dinner plate.

Bock saw the captain squinting at it and told him a Herr Rudolf of Bremerhaven had checked and rechecked the five ship's compasses in his shop, meticulously calculated their deviations, and installed this one himself, noting less than one-eighth of a point difference between the ship's compass readings and the true course.

"Good," Brickenstein said curtly, and held up to the gaslight the first page of the crew list: *August Lauenstein, First Officer; Carl Thalenhorst, Second Officer; Otto Tramultz, Third Officer; Reinhold Schmidt, Chief Engineer; Siegfried Benning, Ship's Purser; August Bock, Quartermaster; Christian Haase, Quartermaster; Carl Lukermann, Chief Steward; Dietrich Stege, Ship's Carpenter; Dr. Franz Bluen, Chief Physician; Charles Dore Harvey, Pilot.* Brickenstein halted his reading. "Who is this Harvey? British?"

"The English Channel navigator," Lauenstein said. "He'll take command after we reach the Thames estuary, near Owers."

Within the last few years there had been nineteen German ships that wrecked off the hazardous coasts of England and five that had foundered. Wreckage itself was a cause of shipwreck. The isle of Great Britain was considered a graveyard.

"I haven't met him," Brickenstein said.

"Well, he tells me this will be his one-hundred-twenty-first trip."

The captain glanced at two other pages that were filled with the names of the other seamen and crew, many of them familiar to him from his eight years with North German Lloyd. Stuffing the list into his suitcoat pocket, he asked, "Are you staying up for the cargo loading?"

Both August Bock and August Lauenstein agreed that they were.

"Then I'm going down to my quarters," Brickenstein said.

Bock grinned at Lauenstein after he'd gone. "So perhaps our captain *does* sleep."

•

Sister Henrica checked with a Lloyd's agent and discovered there would be no Catholic priest on the ship—a great disappointment—but she found a church with an eight o'clock Saturday-morning Mass that the five could reach on foot. She permitted the Sisters to sleep until six-thirty on December 4th, and when they gathered in Sister Henrica's hotel room, she reminded them that it was the feast day of Saint Barbara. Sister Aurea grinned up at the masculine nun of that name as Sister Henrica told them Saint Barbara had been brought up a heathen in the Middle Ages by a cruel and tyrannical father who jealously kept her holed up in a lonely tower he'd constructed for that purpose. There in her forced solitude the girl studied the Christian mysteries and contrived to receive instruction and baptism by stealth from a priest. Upon discovering his holy daughter's conversion, the father was irate and denounced her as a sorcerer before a civil tribunal. The judges' sentence was that Saint Barbara was to be pitilessly tortured and at last beheaded with an ax. Her own father, merciless to the last, acted as her executioner.

Sister Barbara just stared ahead, stern as a fence post, as Sister Brigitta teared up and held a hand to her mouth.

"Oh, but that is not the end," Sister Henrica said, "for the hagiographers tell us that the Almighty dealt speedily with the holy girl's persecutors. Even while her soul was being borne by the seraphim up to Paradise, a flash of lightning struck down her father, and he was hauled by the scruff of his neck before the judgment seat of God." She paused. "Shall we pray?"

The five bowed their heads.

"Sister Barbara?"

Sister Barbara said, "May we be spared a sudden death that we are unprepared for, and may we be strengthened by Christ and his saints against the horrors and anxieties of our last hour."

And then Sister Barbara led them in singing an "Ave Maria."

•

She was born March 18th, 1843, in the Westphalian village of Deleke, twenty miles west of Salzkotten, the first daughter of the shoemaker Eberhard Hültenschmidt and his wife, Anna Marie. The infant was baptized Anna Gertrud in Saint Pankratius Church in Körbecke on the next day, but in order to distinguish between the two Annas in the house, she was soon called Thecla, the name Eberhard wanted all along.

Even as a child Thecla Hültenschmidt was not like the other girls. She disliked their dolls, their silliness, their pretend housekeeping, their squealing. She shocked them with loudness, restlessness, wild energy. In America she would have been called a tomboy. She was frank and tactless, often baffled that she'd hurt a friend's feelings, and just as often at a loss for words. And so she grew stony and quiet and sought aloneness in the woods, so that her unpretty face was painted with windburn, her red hands were hard, scratched, and chapped. She inherited her father's height and throughout her schooling was often a head taller than many boys, and her body did not halt its horrifying inching upward until at sixteen she'd reached six foot two. Rangy and sinewy—horsey, she thought—she was good at sports, but she could not sit self-effacingly without hunching, and she felt hideous when she danced, with her huge shoes clobbering the floor and some juvenile's head squarely facing her chest or frowning up at her faint mustache.

Reading bored her, but Thecla was shrewd enough in examinations to graduate from a technical high school, then helped out in the shoe shop with a hard-bitten father who could praise no one, who seemed to seek out mechanical objects to punish with his anger. It was her mother who forced her into social occasions with large, kindly, earnest farmers whose little free time was lost in the hunt for a wife. She found those Sunday meetings passably friendly if formal, an hour or two of coffee and cake filled with male factuality and some sincere questioning about Fräulein Hültenschmidt's hobbies and kitchen skills, before she or the man tired of their intercourse and mentioned chores that needed attention, their peaceable afternoon concluding with a handshake and the stiff cordiality of disinterest. She'd watch them shamble away like yoked bullocks and she'd wonder why they found the greater freedom of men such a burden.

And then she attended a Sunday Mass that changed her life. Thecla was nineteen, the man beside her three years older, their heights the same, their hands alike, the timbre of her voice in the sung Latin hymns just a slight tone higher than his baritone, and he a farrier. She fancied that only the intricate braiding of her chestnut-brown hair, the soft mounds of her breasts, and the wider hips underneath her skirt hinted at a femininity she considered wholly fraudulent and one of nature's mistakes. She wakened from distraction when she heard the pastor forget his sermon and recall a second-century Christian legend he'd just read that was called *Acta Pauli et Theclae*.

Thecla, he told the congregation, was a Greek virgin living in Iconium, and she was engaged to be married when she first heard the Apostle Paul preaching about virtue and vice. Won over by Saint Paul's call to continence, Thecla immediately asked to be baptized, saying, "Only give me this holy seal in Christ and trial shall not touch me."

Worried that she was not yet truly aware of the perils of conversion, the Apostle said, "Be patient and learn Christ's teachings, then you shall receive his living water." Soon after that, the pastor said, Thecla became Saint Paul's disciple and, until she was martyred, was justly renowned for her purity and her ability to heal the sick. "Who thinks of Thecla now?" the pastor said. "Yet her name was known, time was, next whitest after Mary's own. And she is still considered the mother of all maidens and nuns."

Thecla Hültenschmidt stewed over that until the Consecration, when she was surprised by tears of joy and assurance streaming down her face. She received Communion with a humility and gratitude that she'd despised seeing in the pious, and she was waiting in the sneering cold outside the sacristy when the shorter pastor was hurrying across to the rectory for coffee and pastries with his housekeeper and curate. She hindered him and hesitantly said, "Monsignor, I think I have a vocation."

She'd not been particularly religious until then, so he stopped and skeptically stared up at her solemn face. "I misheard you," he said.

She held her headscarf tight at her neck and hugged her wool coat closer. "I feel called," she said. "To the convent." And then she quoted an earlier sermon on Saint Irenaeus that she remembered: "Only there can I be fully alive."

"You have just now made this discovery?"

"But still I'm sure of it."

She was told to pray about it and attend daily Mass for six months, and then to meet with the pastor if she felt confirmed in her calling. She did as she was told, she twice was interviewed by him, and soon it was just a matter of choosing the proper religious order. Assessing the pros and cons of each, which seemed a happy pastime for the priest, they mutually agreed she ought to apply to a new foundation of religious women who called themselves Sisters of Saint Francis, Daughters of the Sacred Hearts of Jesus and Mary.

With her parents she rode in the finery she generally avoided from their village of Deleke to the parish church in Salzkotten in a phaeton drawn by two horses, and on a Sunday in October 1865 Thecla Hültenschmidt was among fifteen postulants who were received into the order by Mother Clara Pfänder.

Their motherhouse was then on the east side of Salzkotten on the recently acquired Grundhoff estate, its white stucco, thatch-roofed barn converted into a cold, rude chapel that was still pungent with the scent of cattle, its white-stucco half-timbered mansion now crowded with a dozen orphan children and forty-four nuns. She loved it there: the hours of silence, the children and walking sick whom she cared for, the orderly regimen of their days, the many occasions for prayer.

At first Franciscan poverty was a hardship, with no money for heating coal and with meager meals of hard rolls and black coffee, except for their main noontime dinners, which included jarred vegetables and potatoes. She was continually hungry and thin as a nail, but she gloried in jobs that required her strength, and in the hushed company of women she found her height and masculinity not just tolerated but admired. She stood out and it suited her. And she was thrilled when, a year later, she received the habit and was told her vow name would be Barbara—not because the saint was executed by her own tyrannical father, but because she learned the name was derived from the Latin word for "wild, rough, and savage."

Owing to her high school education in the sciences, Sister Barbara was one of those chosen by Mother Clara for medical and midwife training by Dr. Damm, and in the Franco-Prussian War of 1870–1871, she was among the sixty other nursing Sisters from Salzkotten who were enlisted to serve the needs of the German Army. She assisted in the triage tents at Mars-la-Tour, ministering to shelled infantrymen or those shot down from shocking distances by the new bolt-action long-range chassepot rifle, the crude medicine of the period generally confining Sister Barbara's first aid to tying off blood loss with tourniquets and helping hold victims down as surgeons amputated ruined extremities with a hacksaw. At Gravelotte a photograph was taken of a happy Sister Barbara in a white nurse's apron, sitting on a hospital bed surrounded by twelve smiling soldiers, the legless leaning on crutches, the handless hiding the fact with slings. After the war, she traveled as far east as Bohemia to nurse in doctorless villages hit by epidemics of cholera, dysentery, smallpox, and typhoid.

She became stoical about her own hunger, health, and sheer exhaustion, but was stricken by the hurts and sufferings of children. At thirty-two she could be a stern, no-nonsense harridan with those she considered fools, but she melted and smiled and cooed with those she called "my little ones," and she was often spied in the orphanage well past midnight, softly creaking a rocking chair and humming a folk lullaby as two thumb-sucking babies slept in her arms. When she was told in the fall of 1875 that she would be exiled to a Catholic hospital in America, she said nothing at first, so Mother Clara wondered if she had any questions. And Sister Barbara solemnly asked, "Will there be children there?"

•

Rough seas were growling along the shore, and flits of snow flew into the Sisters' reddening faces as the five scurried back from the Bremerhaven church Saturday morning, embracing themselves for warmth and crouching out of the wind. The high temperature for December 4th would be thirty-one degrees, but it was then far colder. Three went ahead to the Lloyd's Hall for hot coffee and kaiser rolls, but Sister Henrica stayed with Sister Barbara on a cliffwalk, watching zinc-gray waves with trailing hoods of white rush to the shore, the swell's comb morseling into fine string and tassel before bursting on the rocky spurs of the cove and breaking into white bushes of foam.

"Aren't you cold?" Sister Henrica asked.

"Actually, yes," Sister Barbara said, but she still seemed unready to seek haven. She told Sister Henrica that even with it so icy now, the sea temperature was probably as warm as fifty-two degrees Fahrenheit. Because of the Gulf Stream from the south. She'd read that the seas around England and northwest Europe were sixteen degrees warmer than what they should be for that latitude.

"And here we are without our bathing gowns."

Sister Barbara smiled. "We can go inside."

But other passengers were now going outside to the *Deutschland*, hauling handcarts of steamer trunks and furniture behind them onto the dock, or sidling up the gangway with the heaped bedding, pillows, towels, and porcelain washbasins that were required of the hundred passengers in steerage.

There the great, airless hall of bunk beds in the hull of the ship was partitioned so that females traveling alone were segregated aft, families were in the middle, and males over the age of fourteen slept in the forward section next to the cargo holds. Earlier in the century, passengers had been forced to furnish and cook their own food, but by 1875 the shipping competition was such that North German Lloyd had been forced to lure transatlantic passengers by including full board in the steerage price of one hundred twenty marks. Still, there was as little privacy as in a railway station, and steerage had become the source of so much lurid gossip about humiliations and sexual trespasses that Mother Clara insisted the five Sisters travel in second-class cabins, at the cost of three hundred marks each.

The first- and second-class cabins were on an upper floor,

just beneath the weather deck. Only three passengers were making the voyage to America in first class, which strangely was situated closest to the engine noise, and those three had sole access to the yellow-wallpapered music room and its grand piano. Otherwise, first and second class were similar but for the size of the cabins and the services of the stewards—in first class one was awakened by a steward who softly carried in a silver coffee service and zwieback toast, and at four in the afternoon there was an "interim" with tea and chocolate tortes.

The five Sisters found their way through the chaos of dockside and onto the *Deutschland* just before noon on December 4th, and were greeted by Siegfried Benning, the ship's purser, a wide and buoyant man with a gray walrus mustache who'd been handling financial accounts on the *Deutschland* since its maiden voyage nine years earlier. Once he'd confirmed the spelling of their names on his passenger list, he handed out numbered keys to three second-class cabins to the stewards hauling their five black portmanteaus. Sister Brigitta and Sister Aurea would be sharing one cabin, Sister Barbara and Sister Norberta another, and Sister Henrica, their Superior in America, was given the precedence of sleeping alone.

Emigrants from Bohemia who spoke little German were cattling up the gangway behind Quartermaster Bock, who was guiding them to steerage, his white handkerchief wafted high overhead, so Sister Henrica stood off to the side with the ship's purser and furtively handed over the coin purse containing their wealth so she would have no worries about it. Siegfried Benning scrupulously totaled the marks, noted the amount in his ledger, and tagged the coin purse before including it with many others in his lockbox. A lockbox that would be lost at sea.

Captain Brickenstein sidestepped by them, politely tipping his hat to the nuns, and avoided a clutch of relatives weepily hugging their farewells as he headed toward the stern and the six flights of iron stairway that took him down to the engine room. Looking into the hot stokehold, he yelled a hello to three shirtless stokers shoveling coal into a furnace. They grimly nodded, and he withdrew into a slightly cooler engine room that was as huge as a gymnasium.

Chief Engineer Reinhold Schmidt stood up from his paperwork at an oak desk as soon as he saw the new captain, and he conducted him on a tour of the insulated pipes and machinery for the two direct-action steam engines, each as large as a toolshed, and whose capacity, he said, was eighteen hundred horsepower, delivering a service speed of fourteen knots. Schmidt mentioned six-foot inverted cylinders with a four-foot stroke, Krupp's crankshafts, surface condensers, and variable expansion gear, but he soon noticed Captain Brickenstein was without questions and understood that his visit was a formality. "She was fully inspected in dry dock during September," Schmidt said.

"And the engines were examined?"

"Of course."

The captain was hunting sentences. "And the screw?"

The screw was a cast-iron propeller with three blades, each the size of a man, and because such things failed or locked up or were sheared apart on reefs, ships of that period carried sails as supplements. Ships with multiple screws had not yet been constructed. And the auguring action was still so misunderstood that structural defects were engineered into the blades until the twentieth century. But Schmidt assured the captain the *Deutschland*'s only propeller was shipshape.

"Well, then," Captain Brickenstein said.

"We cast off when?"

"Three-thirty."

•

Upstairs in their second-class cabin, Sister Brigitta was unfolding and hanging her other habit in the foot-wide closet as Sister Aurea bounced childishly on the soft mattress of a berth and marveled at the luxury of their surroundings. There were an Axminster rug, scrolls and arabesques in the wallpaper, a gas ceiling light with a green-tasseled, filigreed white globe cover, and a chartreuse-curtained porthole with brass fittings that she could stick her head through if she wanted— and she wanted, but Sister Brigitta said no. She could kick Sister Brigitta's white-painted berth with her dangling shoes, they were that close together, but she'd grown up in a home overplentied with children; she was used to sharing. An upright chest upholstered in green pillows served as a sofa, and underneath it were wide pull-out drawers, and Sister Aurea thought if she still had her dolls she would stow them there, with a facecloth for their sleeping blanket. Hanging above a shining porcelain sink and white Staffordshire pitcher was a gilt-framed, oval mirror that did not warp or vex her face when she peered into it. And a free, lilac-scented bar of soap was aslant on two white bath towels that were as soft to her hands as a sponge.

She asked, "Are the quarters too close for you, Sister Brigitta?"

"They're comfy."

"Wide enough to swing a goose in," Sister Aurea said. "But small enough that the goose would object."

Sister Brigitta smiled.

Sister Aurea told her, "I have stayed in a hotel Thursday night and Friday night, and for the next many days I'll be staying here. No one in Neugarten will believe it."

Sister Brigitta hummed.

"Aren't they nice on this ship?"

Sister Brigitta agreed that they were.

"Which side are we on?"

Sister Brigitta scanned the harbor and she said in English, "The port side." She smiled at Sister Aurea. "Left." She said, "Have you heard the English word 'posh'?"

Sister Aurea's sweet face took on that stupid look, and she dimly shook her head.

"Doctor Damm told me 'posh' means rich, because rich people always voyage on the *port* side going *outward* and the *starboard* side heading *home*."

But Sister Aurea heard only Sister Brigitta's German and the italicizing of *Hafen, auswärts, Steuerbord,* and *Heim.* She was confused.

"It only makes sense in English," Sister Brigitta said.

"Shall we go exploring?"

She scurried ahead of Sister Brigitta to a library of five hundred books where a man in a gray tweed suit was examining nautical maps with his pince-nez, and to a ladies' room that was extravagantly decorated in an Egyptian style, and then to a heated ladies' bathing room with hand-painted medallions of Bremen scenes on the walls, hot water always available, four long, eagle-clawed bathtubs surrounded by rubber curtains, and no rules whatsoever about how often the baths could be used.

"I like the *Deutschland* so much," Sister Aurea said. "Don't you like it, too?"

"Yes, Sister, I do."

"Will there be bathing rooms in Missouri?"

"I have no idea."

"Are there people who speak German there?"

"Certainly. Don't you remember Reverend Brockhagen? He took Sisters Philomena and Mary Dorothea and Alphonsa with him. And there was also Reverend Schindel?"

"Yes."

"With him went Sisters Benedicta, Adolphina, Ida, Ursula, Euphemia, Isadora, Engelberta, and—who else?—Anastasia. And there will be immigrants like us. All the time we'll hear our mother tongue."

Sister Aurea smiled, and then another thought took hold: "Shall we go find the others and tell them about the baths?"

"They know."

"Shall we peek into the gentlemen's bathing room and see what it's like?"

"Sister Aurea!"

"Oh, I was just teasing."

•

She was born in Neugarten in Upper Silesia, on February 26th, 1852, and was baptized Josepha Badziura. She belonged to a people called *Wasserpolacken*, or Water Poles, whose strong and stalwart men Otto von Bismarck recruited for his Prussian Guard in Berlin. Bernice Badziura, Josepha's mother, was almost continually pregnant from the age of seventeen and suffered three miscarriages in the course of giving birth to twelve children, nine of whom survived infancy. Gunter Badziura, Josepha's father, was a stout stevedore who had worked on barges on the Oder River before injuries caused him to hire on as a machinist in Neugarten, where he died of overwork when his youngest daughter was fourteen.

She'd been such a round, placid, and perpetually smiling baby that for some months the little girl's grandparents worried that she might be simple. She rolled rather than crawled, and she still babbled in high-pitched happiness when other children of twenty months were forming sentences. But it turned out that it was just her nature to be unhurried and serene. Any touch was a tickle to little Josepha, and in school she often struggled not to giggle at the lessons. She was held back one grade in *Volksschule* just because she was so much tinier than the other children, and she did not finish high school. She instead took a job as a scullery maid in a parish convent of Dominican nuns, sectioning fruit and peeling potatoes and entertaining the cooks. Monsignor Schwacha told Josepha's mother he could always tell when Josepha was in the kitchen because whenever he strolled the gardens with his breviary, he would hear howls of laughter from the nuns.

When Josepha was nineteen, Sister Theodora, a cook, was mincing onions when she told the scullery maid about Chapter 43 in the Book of Isaiah, where the prophet recorded, "But now thus saith the LORD that created thee, O Jacob, and he that formed thee, O Israel, Fear not: for I have redeemed thee, I have called thee by thy name; thou art mine." And she encouraged Josepha to pray in order to know by what name she was called.

Josepha woke up the next morning with the certainty that God had named her "Little One."

Upon that report, Sister Theodora felt called to immediately escort Josepha to the Dominican library and write out verses in the gospels that spoke of littleness. Jesus, for instance, once told his audience, "Verily I say unto you, Except ye be converted, and become as little children, ye shall not enter into the kingdom of heaven." Jesus told his disciples, "Fear not, little flock; for it is your Father's good pleasure to give you the kingdom." Jairus sought out Jesus, saying, "My little daughter lieth at the point of death: I pray thee, come and lay thy hands on her, that she may be healed; and she shall live." Jesus taught: "Whosoever shall offend one of these little ones that believe in me, it is better for him that a millstone were hanged about his neck, and he were cast into the sea." And he later said, "Even so it is not the will of your Father which is in heaven that one of these little ones should perish."

Josepha was thrilled by the many connections, and she memorized the handwritten passages. And though an older man named Werner who hammered rivets in a local factory had long been courting her in a parental, earnest, and desultory way, calling Josepha his sunshine and sugarplum and sweetmeat, she finally told him she could not marry him, and it soon seemed only natural that she should investigate religious life. She ruled out the Dominicans because they were essentially an intimidating order of teachers, choosing instead the Sisters of Saint Francis, Daughters of the Sacred Hearts of Jesus and Mary, because she'd heard their primary mission was helping orphaned children—little ones—and because Sister Theodora had given her as a Christmas present the book *Fioretti, or The Little Flowers of Saint Francis*.

In her first interview with the foundress at Salzkotten, she'd confessed, "I'm not very smart."

Mother Clara said, "I'm sure you're as smart as you need to be."

"I have this squeaky voice, like I'm five years old."

Mother Clara just smiled.

"I forget things. And I get distracted. My mother says I'm unruly."

"Twenty is not very old. You have years to mature."

She shyly admitted, "I have committed sins against chastity."

Mother Clara gently stared, construing the girl's meaning. "And have you sinned with one man or with many?"

"Oh! Oh no! Only Werner."

"Is this Werner still courting you?"

She shrugged. "I'm not in love with him."

"Will our vow of chastity be difficult for you?"

"Yes. I think it will be really hard."

"Well, you're quite right," Mother Clara said. "It *is* hard. But not impossible. And there *are* compensations."

"Such as the jewelry and fancy dresses?"

Mother Clara's face was stern. "Tell me: Are you trying to convince me *not* to accept you?"

Josepha shoved her hands under her thighs and waggled her feet with nervousness.

"Well, you are failing," Mother Clara said.

She smiled. "Oh, failing is what I'm good at."

On May 21st, 1872, Josepha entered the congregation, and on November 7th she received the habit and the name of Saint Aurea, a holy Syrian abbess and miracle worker who had died of the plague in Paris in 667. She was glad she was not given a man's name.

She became a delight to the older nuns and was thought a friendly, jesting, self-deprecating child by even those her own age. She became nimble at hand embroidery, she was justly praised for her streusels, apple kuchen, and Schwarzwalder tortes, she entertained the children with silly jokes, and she heedlessly disobeyed the Rule with such frequency that it seemed only normal that Sister Aurea would be doing a penance facedown on the floor of the chapel or refectory. But there was no flaunting or scheming or stubbornness in her; she seemed just a wild puppy that needed to be house-trained. And she was impossible to dislike. In November 1875, Conrad Martin, the Bishop of Paderborn, was presented a list of those heading from Salzkotten to America, and when he noticed Sister Aurea's name among the five, he wondered in a letter to the foundress why a housekeeping nun who was still under temporary vows was included among those with such evident skills. Mother Clara tartly wrote back, "Cooking. And for the good of the community."

•

Strolling through second class on the *Deutschland*, Sister Aurea became an extroverted child, gaily introducing herself and Sister Brigitta to Lina and Nisette Schäffer, mother and daughter, both from Philadelphia; to Babette Binder, who would die along with her child; and to Mrs. Anna Gmolch, who would survive the shipwreck, and her little daughter Paulina, who died in her mother's arms on board the rescue boat *Liverpool*. Anna told the nuns she, too, was taking up residence in America, and that her husband had gone before her to rent a flat in Brooklyn and find work in a haberdashery on Seventh Avenue. Mr. and Mrs. William B. Fundling, their daughter Bertha, and their son Theodor halted their unpacking to chat about a happy fortnight visiting relatives in Dortmund and Hannover and to say they were heading back for the Christmas rush in New York City, where Herr Fundling ran a perfumery business on Front Street. Also in second were Procupi Papolkoff, a stereotype of a bearish Russian in a wide sable coat and tall sable hat; a shy Maria Forster from Fritzlar; a Mrs. Hamm, who seemed jailed with a squalling five-month-old baby and a whining five-year-old son; and Edward Stamm and his six-year-old daughter, Elise, whom he patted on the head as he confessed she spoke no German, having grown up in Texas.

Sister Brigitta smiled at the little girl and said in English, "Zo, in the Lone Star State you . . ." She forgot the verb and looked to Elise's father. *"Wohnen?"*

"Reside," said Edward Stamm in English.

The girl just stared, and Sister Brigitta lost the nerve to continue.

Of the three passengers in first class, the Sisters met only Carl Dietrich Meyer, from Westfalen, a hearty businessman who seemed familiar with Roman Catholicism but called them *Fräulein* and slyly assayed Sister Brigitta's form and beauty before acceding to Sister Aurea's request and, his hands familiarly riding their backs, escorted them past a scowling stewardess to the music room. Centered in it was a gleaming black Julius Blüthner grand piano on which Sister Aurea plinked a five-note children's tune as Sister Brigitta's hands lovingly passed over the elegant yellow jacquard fabric on the sofas. She recalled the cultivation and luxury of the lawyer Wilhelm Tiltmann's house. She was certain he would have married her and she'd be in Lippstadt now, with fineries and servants and children perhaps. And yet she'd chosen this odd, hard life of denial.

Sidling over, Carl Dietrich Meyer cozily inquired of Sister Brigitta, "And do you play as well?"

Sister Brigitta called to Sister Aurea, "We should go."

"Oh, please no!" Herr Meyer said. "Lovely girls, please stay! There are only three of us in first class. I'll be so lonely."

"Some other time," Sister Brigitta said. And in the hallway she told Sister Aurea, "Don't do that to me."

Sister Aurea grinned. "And *do* you play, Sister Brigitta?"

"No," she said. "I do not."

•

At three on Saturday afternoon, August Lauenstein was out on the weather deck of the *Deutschland*. Holding his white first officer's hat to his head in the frantic wind, he stood underneath the mainmast and supervised the raising of the North German Lloyd company flag, its snapping white field displaying laurel sprigs of periwinkle blue wreathed in the middle of a crossed blue anchor and old-fashioned key. On the foremast the Bremen ensign was already furling, but he thought it stupid and cruel in such weather to send a seaman up the rigging to untangle it. Soon, when they were under way, Lauenstein would hoist off the stern the federal black, white, and red *Bundesflag* of Germany, and then he could sneak down to his quarters and sink into a hot bath of sleep as the Weser River pilot took the helm.

Lauenstein was sixty and no longer spry; a tall, hardused, skeletal man with skin as crosshatched with wrinkles as an elephant's flesh, and with stern, silvery eyes that seemed to stab whatever he saw. At thirteen he'd joined the Navy as a cadet and was a midshipman when at nineteen he was drummed out of the service for a mysterious incident of violence on a shore leave in Yalta. Over his next forty-one years on merchant ships, he'd lost a toe to frostbite, three finger joints to dockyard accidents, and some teeth to an illness that was possibly scurvy; and he was still so thin from his last bout with dysentery that he could number all his bones. There had been hard winters on the *Hammonia* of the Hamburg-America line when he and his maintenance crew were required to carry out continuous repairs as the overmatched mail steamer struggled in high seas, and he once was so exhausted that he fell into unconsciousness while tying his shoes.

In late middle age, August Lauenstein passed his "Master of Vessels" exam, but by then his father and two other relatives had lost their lives in various shipwrecks and Lauenstein found himself reluctant to assume the solemn responsibilities of captaincy. So it was as a quartermaster that he hired onto the *Bremen*, North German Lloyd's first Atlantic steamer, and he did not become a first officer, or mate, until after the Franco-Prussian War, when Captain Ludewigs sought him for that position on the *Deutschland*.

On shore Lauenstein rented a heatless attic room above a Bremerhaven gasthaus and, depressed that his wealth of life was spent, lost himself and his money in weeks-long drunkenness with now-and-then friends who were sprat fishermen. And then there would come a time when the owner shouted "August!" and shook him awake in his booth and told him he was to ship out again. Immediately he pretended responsibility, had his clothing spruced and his white hair scissored short as a crew cut, waxed his wide, gull-winged mustache, and became not just sober and respectable but, on his own terms, chipper.

And so he was smiling as he watched Sister Henrica stroll the long field of the weather deck in her cloak and mittens. Contained in prayer. Absorbed by the rosary beads she was thumbing. Lauenstein ordered a seaman to tighten the halyards and went aft to the pilothouse.

Sister Henrica felt herself tilt a little as she strolled, and realized there was a slight camber to the weather deck, so that seawater would slosh to the port and starboard sides of the ship and into the scuppers along the rail. Otherwise the ship's surface was as flat as a street in Cologne but for the pilot-house, the fenced funnel and giant masts, and just a foot off the floor the twelve shining windowpanes of a skylight that could be hoisted open on chains for sea air. She bent to gaze through it to the great room below, which she'd heard called the saloon. A five-year-old boy whom she'd learn was Adam Schwartz, from Schweigen in Baden, looked up and smiled as he waved hello, and Sister Henrica waved back. Jacobine Schwartz, the boy's mother, hotly whispered into his ear and his face fell. Sister Henrica withdrew from the mother's criticism and strolled toward the *Deutschland*'s stern.

Seamen shouted to each other in their hectic work on the ship and dock, and many passengers were rushing up from steerage in order to watch the launch. She noticed on the weeded landslips of the shore that zephyrs were scudding little clouds of the morning's snow-dust and the fine flakes sparkled in the sun as they rose. Along the dock the snow was gliding over the tarred planks in white wisps that between trailing and flying shifted and wimpled like so many silvery worms.

She was found by Sister Aurea and the others, and the five joined a crowd near the stern as the gangways were hauled up, the heavy hawser lines were lifted off their mooring posts, and three tugboats started towing the *Deutschland* out into the harbor. Watching the Bremerhaven quay recede, Sister Henrica was the victim of sentimental sorrow and self-pity and could not help but weep, for she was certain she would never see her father or siblings or homeland again. The four

Sisters closed around her with tears sliding from their eyes and held each other by the waist as they sang *"Das Lied der Deutschen,"* whose lyrics began *"Deutschland, Deutschland, über Alles."* Soon all on the weather deck were singing the republic's anthem, and when it was finished, the five Sisters wiped their cheeks and hugged each other. And Sister Aurea told Sister Henrica, "Christ was an exile, too. Wasn't he?"

And Sister Henrica said, "Yes, I think so."

•

Captain Brickenstein was in the pilothouse, seriously watching his sniveling passengers, who seemed unconscious of the superstition that it was bad luck to look back once a ship has left port. August Lauenstein was an old tavern mate of the Weser River pilot at the helm and fawned over his friend's new A. Lange & Söhne oversized wristwatch as they oversaw the three tugboats and noted that there were reports of worsening weather ahead. Captain Brickenstein turned from the intermittent sunshine of Bremerhaven to a high gray wall of mist looming over the Weser estuary, which was called the *Helgoländer Bucht.* And with nightfall so early in December, in fact in less than an hour, the Weser pilot thought it might be wisest to halt near the harbor lightship until sunrise, the pilot needlessly adding, "I have only my eyes to go by, after all."

And so it was that the *Deutschland* dropped its chained starboard anchor at the mouth, or *Bucht,* of the wide Weser estuary in thirty fathoms of water—one hundred eighty feet—and Saturday night was spent off the coast of Wremen, a town on the eastern shore of the Weser River that was no more than ten miles distant from the Bremerhaven dock-yards. But in a voyage estimated at eleven days and thirteen hours, such a delay was not considered crucial.

•

The five Sisters sang the plainchant of Vespers in their Superior's cabin on Saturday evening and ventured to the dining hall at seven. The chief steward introduced himself as Herr Carl Lukermann and seated the Sisters at a round table that could accommodate ten patrons, so the five were joined there by the Russian Procupi Papolkoff, who seemed rather drunk and carried with him a milk glass of vodka, and by Otto Tramultz, the genial, gray-bearded third officer on the *Deutschland*, who would not survive the coming ordeal. Walking behind him was the ship's chief physician, Dr. Franz Bluen, whose ribbons of white hair were intricately woven over his otherwise bald head. And then the chief steward invited over a handsome farm boy named Adolf Hermann and a pretty girl who could have been his younger sister but was Anna Petzold, whose relatives in Bremen had convinced him to escort the girl to her home in New York City and "see that no harm befalls her." Adolf grinned as he confessed to Sister Henrica that Anna was eighteen, just three years younger than he, she spoke good German, and she was not after all *that* ugly, so he thought a two-week voyage with the girl might not be such a hardship. Anna's face flushed with the flattery, and Sister Henrica wondered if Adolf knew the girl was already in love with him.

The dinner menu was enclosed in blond Italian leather and featured a first course of oxtail soup, then either a fish course of turbot or lobster or a meat course of mutton cutlets or venison. Sauerkraut, potatoes, and canned asparagus were

offered as side dishes, and dessert was Limburger or Emmen-
thaler cheese. Sister Brigitta held her cheeks in shock as she
read the menu. In Salzkotten she'd be dining on only a cold
bread roll and vegetable soup. "It's so much!" she exclaimed.
"It's overwhelming!"

Sister Henrica explained to Tramultz, "We usually have
our main meal at noon."

"We, too," the third officer said. "But we had the afternoon launch, and the officers and hands were too busy to eat."

"And everyone wants his money's worth," said Dr. Bluen.

"Quite right," Tramultz said and snapped his fingers
overhead. A peeved sommelier wandered over to help with
choices of Rhine, Pfalz, or Mosel wine.

Waiting for their food, Otto Tramultz sought to entertain
the diners by proudly relating that he was one of seventeen
crew members on the *Germania* during Captain Karl Kol-
dewey's 1869 expedition to the North Pole. They'd explored
and mapped the eastern coast of Greenland, harbored for the
winter—"In September!" he said—in a bay of Sabine Island,
and mushed sled dogs on overland journeys to a latitude as
far north as seventy-seven degrees. Imagine it, nine hundred
miles farther north than they were now. Almost to the top of
the world. It was a fifteen-month expedition, he told them, in
the direst weather he'd ever felt, and he still had all his fingers
and toes.

"I hate getting cold," Sister Aurea said. And Sister Henrica secretly but strictly wagged a finger, for the word "hate"
was forbidden them.

"Oh, the cold!" Otto Tramultz exclaimed, and he told
them they couldn't imagine it. "Lose a glove in the snow and
you'd do horrible damage to your hand before you could pick

it up again. Coffee would cool on the short trip from kettle to cup. On Sabine Bay a local boy fell off a schooner and nobody even tried to save him because no one could survive more than a minute in water as cold as that."

Sister Norberta thought he was exaggerating and said so.

But Dr. Franz Bluen defended the third officer with medical science, telling them a sudden plunge into such cold water would cause a gasp expelling almost the entire air volume from the lungs. In some instances, the heart immediately stops. One dies. In others, there is an involuntary and sixfold increase in inhalations, as in a state of panic, which induces thrashing about. And since water conducts heat faster than air, swimming and treading water and such other natural responses actually increase heat dispersal. Seek air to breathe and more heat is lost through the head. The extremities contract into a fetal crouch to protect the furnace of the heart, but skin and neighboring tissues cool very fast, and soon internal core temperatures drop below ninety degrees, prompting loss of consciousness or the inability to use one's arms and legs. And *then*, if not earlier, the heart stops. Even the strongest swimmers could manage no more than a mile in the cold waters of the North Sea before being overcome by hypothermia and dying.

The Russian, the young people, and the five Sisters just stared at him as he concluded and then permitted the service of the oxtail soup. But Sister Norberta asked him, "Why is it you smile when you relate such awful things?"

Dr. Bluen was embarrassed. "I'm so sorry. I simply love science."

"The fishermen off Greenland?" Otto Tramultz said. "They don't even try learning to swim. What's the use?"

"The soup looks good," Sister Barbara said.

"Oxtail," Dr. Bluen told her, and spooned some.

"You're the tall one," the Russian drunkenly told Sister Barbara, as if she hadn't noticed. Sister Barbara stared without emotion. And he stabbed his forefinger toward Sister Aurea. "She's the short one."

Correcting him, she said, "Little one."

Papolkoff grinned. "See, I don't need names, do I?" Winking, he said of Sister Brigitta, "The pretty one. Am I right?"

Sister Brigitta reddened.

"Sir, you are taking liberties," Dr. Bluen said.

"Oh, where is your sense of humor?"

Sister Henrica softly cautioned the Russian with Aesop: "Clumsy jesting is no joke."

But he just tapped his skull for Dr. Bluen. "She's the smart one. I could tell it from the first instant."

Otto Tramultz told Sister Henrica, "I'm very sorry for this, Sister. Shall I have him removed?"

She shook her head.

Sister Norberta's fury was such that she almost lunged as she demanded of the Russian, "And what am I?"

Procupi Papolkoff was stymied for a moment, and then feebly tried, "Angry?"

•

She was born in Steinsdorf, in Upper Silesia, now Poland, on May 21st, 1845, the third pitiful non-son of the tenant farmer Joseph Reinkober and his wife, Veronika. She was baptized Johanna on the very next day, because she was hardly the size of her father's hand and was not expected to live. But she did, and at Christmas that year Johanna's parents knelt with the baby at the Communion rail and solemnly promised their miracle child to the service of Christ in the Church.

She grew up with the recognition that she was a gift to God, and even as a toddler Johanna would halt whatever she was doing and gaze with such wide-eyed amazement at nuns that her mother once gave her a birthday gift of a gray habit and veil. Frau Reinkober was stunned when the child insisted on wearing it all the time, and she finally had to hide it beneath her husband's woolen underclothes in their chiffonier.

Johanna felt special, and that specialness could make the girl as fretful, indulged, nasty, and pigheaded as a queen. She was jealously devoted to her father and lofty with her mother. She ruled her older sisters with wild threats and tantrums. She could not lose at games without crying. She blamed teachers for what she did not learn, and blamed noise, heredity, and dull weather for the lingering and ever-recurring headaches, influenzas, and lung congestions that kept her out of school. She was fat but frail, quarrelsome but pious, whining but conscience-smitten, and melancholy over any exertion to offer her solace or joy.

Johanna was seventeen when she first applied to join a religious order as a postulant, but she did not interview well: she told them she would do no housekeeping; she could not sing; these were the foods she ate. Entreaties for candidacy that were answered by cordial invitations were in turn answered by Johanna's insulting questions about the quality of instruction, the heating in the motherhouse, the order's fidelity to Rome.

She was twenty-one and still living at home—five feet ten inches tall, ash blond, overweight, ordinary of face, as well as friendless and loveless, a "spoiled vocation," ironing other people's laundry for pfennigs—when she overheard her father tell his wife how worried he was about Johanna. "She's become impossible," he said.

Weeks later he was dead—he just failed to wake up one morning, as if overcome with weariness—and she felt she was responsible. She tearfully prayed at his funeral that he intercede for her in Heaven, help her change whatever she could, and fill up with godliness all that was lacking in herself. She wanted to become possible again.

Ever so gradually Johanna did change, and on June 20th, 1868, at age twenty-three, she was received into the Third Order of Saint Francis as an extern, meaning she was connected to a Steinsdorf convent but did not reside in it. And when, four years later, she asked to join Mother Clara's foundation as a postulant, a pastor could write of her: "This testimonial certifies that this person always conducted herself in a praiseworthy manner, diligently attended the parish Mass, frequently received the Sacraments during the year, and above all distinguished herself by her religious conviction and modest way of life."

Johanna Reinkober entered Salzkotten òn March 15th, 1872, and on November 7th she received the habit and the name Norberta. The name was from the Old German for "blond hero," and was a feminization of Saint Norbert. Though he'd founded an international religious order called the Norbertines, she'd never heard of him. On the night of her vows, she snuck off to the motherhouse library and learned that Norbert was royalty in the twelfth century, and that he cynically received Holy Orders as a savvy career move, but a close call with death initiated a deep and heartfelt conversion. Wandering Europe as a mendicant, and stirring souls with his spellbinding preaching and saintly example, Norbert helped reform monastic houses, worked tirelessly to restore dignity and integrity to the priesthood, and became the famously affable and delightful archbishop of Magdeburg, in Saxony-Anhalt, where he died in 1134.

Like many other nuns, Sister Norberta marveled that while she would never have chosen a masculine name for herself, she realized, now that it was assigned, that here was a hero fit for her, and a holy man she felt certain she resembled.

3

ALLEGIANCE

With theology classes and examinations concluded, Hopkins passed the morning of December 24th in private prayer and outdoor recreation, joining those Jesuit scholastics skating the corrugated ice on a brook. But Hopkins became so fascinated by a kind of Sanskrit in the ice itself that he fell to his knees and crouched over green ice that was like a book of slow freezing, his face inches away in his reading of jots and bursts and traceries that he considered exquisitely beautiful.

"Are you all right there, Hop?" Gavin called.

Hopkins faintly waved a hand but stayed hunched in his enthralled scrutiny. And he smiled as he heard Rickaby shout, "Oh, it's just another of his salaams to nature."

•

Oyster stew and shellfish were served at the main dinner, and then the hours of afternoon were devoted to crafting gifts for someone in the community. Hopkins was given the name of Brother James McKeon, the refectorian, a sort of cook and restaurant manager, and he painted an Alps scene on a little box that would hold McKeon's foxed and food-stained recipe cards.

With the luxury of time, Hopkins also wrote a Christmas letter to "My Dearest Mother," thanking her for the gifts she'd sent, thanking his sister Kate for a mailing, congratulating his youngest brother, Everard, for artwork published in the journal *Iced Tea*, and returning to his sister Grace a school paper she'd written on Nicholas Breakspear, the twelfth-century Augustinian abbot who became Pope Adrian IV, and whose writing style struck Hopkins as a "great babble," for "he cannot say a plain thing in a plain way (I believe musical people never can)."

And then the Jesuit noted his obligation to his mother for some newspaper cuttings:

> Nevertheless you made two oversights. You sent two duplicates, for one thing, and the other was that you omitted the most interesting piece of all, the account of the actual shipwreck: the wreck of the *Deutschland*, 7 Dec. 1875. One or more of the cuttings may have come from the *Illustrated London News*. The issue of 18 Dec. w double-page drawing, "Wreckers at work in the saloon of the Deutschland," and another, "Wreck of the Deutschland as it appeared in the morning of Thursday week." There is also a drawing, "Rescue of the survivors of the Deutschland by the Harwich steam-tug Liverpool": fortunately I had read it but still I should have been glad to have had it by me to refer to again, for I am writing something on this wreck, which may perhaps appear but it depends on how I am speeded. It made a deep impression on me, more than any other wreck or accident I ever read of.
>
> My gas does flicker but I have ceased to care for it or notice it. My neighbour has got a new burner, lucky for him: it does not perceptibly lessen my light. On the other hand he has lost eight teeth.

Have you guessed the charade in the Xmas *Illustrated*? I
have. Where is Aunt Anne spending her Christmas? and where
Aunt Kate? With the best Christmas wishes to all I remain
your loving son,

GERARD M. HOPKINS, S.J.

•

In that northern latitude sunset occurred just before four
o'clock, and he could look up at the skies and watch the stars
wink like diamonds as he strolled the cold gray lawn with his
rosary. Soon there were bright boroughs of starlight, like the
May-mess of fruit-tree petals on a lawn, and in the constella-
tion of Cancer the Christmas cluster called *Praesepe*—Latin
for the manger from which cattle are fed and in which the
newborn Jesus was laid. He kissed his hand to the stars.
Walking back inside the house through the kitchen entrance,
he smelled the pleasing scents of taffy and mincemeat pies in
the ovens, and grinned at the jokes and greetings of the Irish
cooks, and felt unworthy of such happiness.

That night there was a housewide holiday party with
claret wine and Cheddar cheese. Rector James Jones fascinated them with scenes from Sicily and Italy projected with a
magic lantern; Reverend Henry Edwards, the minister, or
assistant rector, read sentimental selections from Charles
Dickens and George Eliot; one gift each was handed out as
the third-year theologians sang "God Rest Ye Merry, Gentlemen"; and then they all played the American game of a
Spelling Bee, which Dick Clarke, of Saint John's College, Oxford, won, Hopkins having been disgraced near the last by his
misspelling of "allegiance."

Receiving his prize of a stick of taffy, Clarke strolled over
to Hopkins and consoled him with a "Sorry, old chap."

Hopkins smiled. "Oh, it's no first for me," he said. "My allegiances have often been questioned."

•

He was born in Stratford, England, on July 28th, 1844, the eldest of nine children in the upper-middle-class family of Kate and Manley Hopkins. Kate was the daughter of a London doctor, and affectionate, free-spirited, raven-haired, dramatic. She left a girls' school called Brunswick House at sixteen, married seven years later, and by age forty was the eccentric, motherly overseer of a household of twelve family members, a governess, and two servants. Her amusements were magazines, puzzles, charades, and learning the Italian language, which she never mastered. She attended Anglican services as social custom required, and she would insist that Gerard read a chapter of the New Testament each night when he boarded at Highgate School. Kate once posed for a serious photograph in a sloe-black silk gown and long lace shawl, a jeweled opera fan in one hand, looking, as she'd intended, like a Mediterranean diva. She was overly health-concerned, but laughter-loving and self-effacing, and she elicited graciousness from every gentleman she met. She was particularly close to her firstborn son, but piously anti-Catholic and critical of his Jesuit vocation. The sole convert in the family seemed unperturbed by that, and his jaunty, journalistic letters to "My Dearest Mother" usually signed off with "believe me always your loving son, Gerard M. Hopkins, S.J."

His father, Manley, was a wispy, vigorous, dapper man, handsomer than his son, with a middle-parted napkin of auburn hair, looming eyebrows, twinkling blue eyes, and a full mustache that he groomed with a tiny comb after dining. Quitting school at fifteen for financial reasons, though he'd long yearned for higher education at Cambridge or Oxford, Manley would become the owner of a successful firm of marine insurance adjusters and became as well Hawaii's consul general in Great Britain. Ever watchful for a chance at a pun, he entertained his children like a debonair houseguest, and on holidays acted with them in playlets, but he was seldom home from his London office before their bedtime, and could be an ill-at-ease headmaster with his children, criticizing them with silence and sighs—just one of his six sons joined him in the family business. Manley's greatest enthusiasms were literary: practical manuals on insurance and maritime procedure, a history of Hawaii, an unpublished novel, an unproduced play, book reviews in *The Times*, a regular newspaper column in *The Polynesian*, the collection *The Philosopher's Stone and Other Poems*, and, with his brother Marsland, an Anglican priest, the religious poetry of *Pietas Metrica; or, Nature Suggestive of God and Godliness*.

Manley's oldest son, Gerard, was ginger-haired, with gleaming eyes that were the color of hazelnuts, a head that seemed slightly too large for his weedy frame, and a long nose and jutting, cleft chin that he thought were distressingly British. Somewhat effeminate in his voice and manner, he was aware of the irony of his middle name and did not use it, though "manly" would become one of his highest compliments for persons or verse. Stubborn, tenacious, and fearless, as self-disciplined as a practiced ascetic, he was also modest, charming, witty, antic, full of jokes and chaff, loyal in his friendships, and was called by a classmate "the nicest boy" at Highgate School. But he was also stunningly intelligent and incisive, quite certain of his opinions, coolly stinging in his criticisms, and jarred when others felt insulted by the lance of his accurate judgments. Some images of him in photographs are of a languid, frail, ethereal aesthete, and though Hopkins played reckless, uncoordinated cricket in school, he generally avoided sport and was content to watch others skating and rowing, though he regularly took twenty-five-mile hikes, conquered larger men in Indian wrestling, and could climb to the highest limbs of a tree with the ease of someone scaling a ladder.

He and his father sparred with drollery and wordplay and stern corrections of each other. His mother thought him graceful, sensitive, ornery, and continually surprising. His father's sister, Aunt Annie, lived with the household and taught "Gerry" painting, pencil drawing, and music, though he would never become accomplished at either piano or violin. He was a gregarious loner, an entertaining observer, a weather watcher, etymologist, cartoonist, and nature artist who recorded his surveillance in journals.

In them, there was no mention of a girlfriend, a cotillion, or a party. Because his teachers and classmates were pervasively male, the only members of the opposite sex he encountered were his older relatives, his younger sisters, and the household servants. Looking at museum paintings, he avoided those that in British delicacy were called "life studies," feeling conflicted and confused if they were women, and embarrassed and impure if the nudes were men. England in the Victorian era prized an invulnerability to lust in its gentlemen, and it was said of grooms that they approached their wedding night in ignorance, while their virgin brides added to that only terror. Marriage was sentimentally esteemed,

but the expected upper-middle-class standards of house and
staff and child-after-child made marriage financially impossible for some, so it was common in the educated classes to
delay it even into one's forties. At Highgate School and at
Oxford almost all of Hopkins's instructors were bachelors,
and the question of their sexual orientation was never raised.
Early on, Hopkins decided he would imitate them.

At age sixteen, Hopkins won the school poetry prize for
"The Escorial," describing in fifteen stanzas the conquest of a
famous Spanish palace, monastery, and church, and he later
was awarded the Governor's Gold Medal for Latin Verse and
an Exhibition, or partial scholarship, to Oxford. And in
1863, just before he entered Balliol College, his poem "Winter with the Gulf Stream" was published in the national journal *Once a Week*.

The first poems he wrote at Oxford were full of Christian
imagery and themes—a nun's reflections on taking the veil in
"Heaven-Haven," Lenten fasting in "Easter Communion,"
or the penitential self-recriminations in "Myself Unholy." But
they were full, too, of yearning and wistfulness, of the clois-
tered contemplative's comfort in the *via negativa* of self-
denial as when, in "The Habit of Perfection," he fantasized
a future religious life of "Elected Silence," poverty, and asceticism, where, as an Anglican priest, "you shall walk the
golden street / And you unhouse and house the Lord."

As a first-year student interrogating the notion of possible
ordination into the Anglican clergy, Hopkins became involved in the High Church group organized by Reverend
Henry Parry Liddon, who sought to invest English services
with Roman liturgical ritual and to oppose the rationalism
and theological liberalism that was emigrating from Ger-

many. Each Sunday night Hopkins attended Reverend Liddon's "Tea, Toast, and Testament" lectures in Saint Edmund Hall, and in strictest conscience he began recording his sins and scruples in a confessional journal, a habit not unlike the nightly examination of conscience he would later practice as a Jesuit.

And gradually he began considering a religious conversion, for it seemed to him it was the Church of Rome that had given Great Britain so much that was "high, elevating, majestic, affecting, and captivating," while the Church of England, "its very title an offence," had given rise to "religious persecution, the jurisdiction of tyrants, and an Establishment whose highest praise for itself was that it admitted a variety of opinions." Writing to a friend, Hopkins indicated that he felt Roman Catholicism paradoxically intensified and subjectively destroyed what he called the "sordidness of things," and he felt that would be enough inducement to lead many people to the Roman Catholic Church. In an age when theological differences were greatly exaggerated, the legitimacy of Anglican dogma and sacraments, particularly that of High Communion and the prayer of Consecration that omitted the Holy Spirit, became a nagging worry to him; the prosaic Sunday sermons he heard in Oxford chapels filled him with contempt; he thought of religious asceticism and even eternal punishment as ways of correcting the "triviality of this life." He read *Apologia Pro Vita Sua*, John Henry Newman's important autobiographical account of his own gradual shift away from the Church of England, and considered him a kindred spirit. Newman had written that "the exterior world, physical and historical, was but the manifestation to our senses of realities greater than itself. Nature was a parable,

Scripture was an allegory; pagan literature, philosophy, and mythology, properly understood, were but a preparation for the Gospel. The Greek poets and sages were in a sense prophets."

Hopkins's own religious conversion, he later wrote, occurred "all in a minute," and "the happiness it has been the means of bringing me I cd. not have conceived." A friend noted in a vacation journal entry for July 24th, 1866: "Walked out with Hopkins and he confided to me his fixed intention of going over to Rome. I did not attempt to argue with him as his grounds did not admit of argument."

Within a few weeks Hopkins was writing a letter to John Henry Newman at his oratory in Birmingham, saying he was anxious to become a Roman Catholic. "I do not want to be helped to any conclusions of belief," he cautioned, "for I am thankful to say my mind is made up, but the necessity of becoming a Catholic . . . coming upon me suddenly has put me into painful confusion of mind about my immediate duty in my circumstances."

Hiding his intentions from his classmate Robert Bridges, he joined him for a September holiday in the rectory of Bridges's stepfather, an Anglican priest, and was high-strung and temperamental until a postcard inviting him to Birmingham finally found him. The houseguest left immediately, as if he'd been jailed, an incivility he regretted, and was garrulous and agitated when he was greeted by the great man in an oratory parlor.

Dr. Newman was then sixty-five, rail-thin and frail, with white hair that was like a soft cap of snow and a large beak of a nose that seemed, on him, elegant. He was welcoming and charming, but nuanced all his words and actions with the grandeur and eminence of royalty, the wit and intellect of the Oxford professor he had been, and the soothing kindliness of a medical resident. He served pekoe tea to Hopkins, tilted with languor in his Regency chair as he interestedly listened as Hopkins told of his vexations on his holiday with Bridges, and then sought to calm the undergraduate with a genial, grumpy narrative of his own misguided winter in Switzerland.

"The sheer amount of food was unnerving," Newman said in his metronomic, much-esteemed voice. "Something fish-like that was boiled, then a cold lobster salad, a wing of a pigeon, a shoe of hard beef, an impossible sweetbread, some muddle of beans, and, to conclude, some cruel ice. And all of it served at vast intervals, with myself uncertain whether my stomach should be able to manage yet another dish, and my jaws uncooperative. Chewing is, of course, the great secret of food digesting well. And even the finest beds were intolerable, though wonderfully hot. Waking each morning with a crick in my neck, or a pain in my shoulders, or a foot bare. At Champéry I had to lie like a serpent in and out, and the upper mattress was so new and springy—filled with horsehair I was told—that there was no fault to be found with it, except that it murdered sleep."

Eventually the conversation shifted to the problems of Catholics at public universities, and then to the controversies that increasingly greeted each of Newman's continual publications—for it seemed misunderstanding him had become the habit not only of journalists and inveterate enemies but of the Roman Catholic bishops in England who ought to have been his friends.

Without a sigh, Newman said, "Oh well. Authority often

exalts opinions into dogmas and works to destroy every
school of thought but its own. And it may be that I'm out
of joint with the times. Perhaps it's God's will that my writing and intentions only be accepted a hundred years later—
disappointing as it is to be snubbed and stopped in so much
of what I attempt." He sat up straighter to pour more tea into
their cups and then resettled with his left cheek on his fist and
an index finger forcing wider his left ear, an unconscious,
characteristic gesture indicative of a slight hearing loss. "But
enough about me. Would you mind if I questioned you about
this grand adventure of yours?"

Writing to Robert Bridges later, Hopkins noted:

Dr. Newman was most kind, I mean in the very best sense, for
his manner is not that of solicitous kindness but genial and
almost, so to speak, unserious. And if I may say so, he was so
sensible. He asked questions which made it clear for me how
to act; I will tell you presently what that is: he made sure I was
acting deliberately and wished to hear my arguments; when I
had given them and said I cd. see no way out of them, he
laughed and said "Nor can I": and he told me I must come to
the Church to accept and believe—as I hope I do. He thought
there appeared no reason, if it had not been for matters at
home of course, why I shd. not be received at once, but in no
way did he urge me on, rather the other way.

In an October letter to his father, Hopkins explained:

My conversion is due to the following reasons mainly (I have
put them down without order)—(i) simple and strictly drawn
arguments partly my own, partly others', (ii) common sense,

(iii) reading the Bible, especially the Holy Gospels, where texts like 'Thou art Peter' (the evasions proposed for this alone are enough to make one a Catholic) and the manifest position of St. Peter among the Apostles so pursued me that at one time I thought it best to stop thinking of them, (iv) an increasing knowledge of the Catholic system (at first under the form of Tractarianism, later in its genuine place), which only wants to be known in order to be loved—its consolations, its marvellous ideal of holiness, the faith and devotion of its children, its multiplicity, its array of saints and martyrs, its consistency and unity, its glowing prayers, the daring majesty of its claims, etc etc.

Hopkins was accepted into the Roman Catholic Church by Reverend Newman on Sunday, October 21st, 1866. Expatriation might have been received with greater equanimity. Reverend Edward Pusey, a professor of divinity at Oxford, nastily wrote his student that he was a "pervert," the Victorian term for those Queen Elizabeth had called "recusant Catholics." In a letter to Florence Nightingale, Benjamin Jowett, Hopkins's tutor, referred to him as one of "three foolish fellows at our College . . . [who] have gone over to Rome." Manley Hopkins sorrowfully condemned his son for his suddenness, irrationality, and coldness, noting that "the manner in which you seem to repel & throw us off cuts us to the heart." And his shocked mother added in postscript, "O Gerard my darling boy are you indeed gone from me?" With seeming innocence she later would pass along to him whatever unsavory gossip she heard about the Church—inciting only serene instruction and condescension from her son—and the only time she or her husband ever visited him as a Jesuit was when he lay dying in Dublin in 1889.

Benjamin Jowett still called him "the star of Balliol," and in his final examinations in "Greats," Hopkins was awarded First Class Honors—generally the first step toward an enviable career as a professor of classical languages. But as a Catholic at that time he could not be granted a higher degree or fellowship in an Oxford college, and even in external professions in which no religious creed was insisted upon, the English loathing for Roman Catholicism and the centuries-old ordinances against it would be a significant hindrance.

With some reluctance, then, he took a job as a schoolmaster at Dr. John Henry Newman's oratory in Birmingham, a preparatory school for the Catholic gentry, but ordination to the priesthood was still on his mind when he made a five-day Holy Week retreat with Reverend Henry Coleridge—a Jesuit and a convert and the grandnephew of the critic and poet Samuel Taylor Coleridge.

The retreat master spoke of Saint Ignatius's principle of *Agere contra*—Latin for "to do the opposite." Our fallen natures were such, Coleridge said, that our tendencies and instincts were soured by laziness or lust or, the chief enemy of holiness, pride. We consider ourselves exceptional, entitled. And so Saint Ignatius recommended that if one hour of prayer seemed wearisome, to pray for an hour and a half; if fasting on Friday seemed hard, then add Saturday as well. Little by little, the preening and ravenous desires of selfishness and egotism would be conquered by the spirit, and we would be freed of our unhealthy attachments. There was nothing scathing or censorious in Coleridge's talks or in the counsel he offered Hopkins in Confession. Coleridge seemed jocular, at home in the world, wise and realistic and strong; the sort of vigorous, intelligent, laughing man Hopkins had often sought out at Oxford; his heartiness a bit like that of Bridges, but with a healthy piety that the Jesuit was so at ease with that he could scoff at its importance. Hopkins didn't just like him; he wanted to *be* like him.

The consequence of that retreat was that Hopkins resolved to become not just a Catholic priest but—seeking even more constraints—a member of a religious order, and after some intensive discernment over whether it would be that instituted by Saint Benedict or the stricter one of Saint Ignatius, Hopkins predictably chose the latter, and at the age of twenty-four entered the Society of Jesus at the British Province Novitiate in Roehampton, southwest of London, in September 1868.

The Novitiate consisted of two years in which the novices undertook a tiring but illuminating thirty-day retreat of silence, introspection, and meditative prayer based on the *Spiritual Exercises* of Saint Ignatius Loyola, studied hagiographies, spiritual classics, and *The Constitutions of the Society of Jesus and Their Complementary Norms*, spoke only Latin much of the day, worked at the janitorial and gardening tasks that were called *manualia*, visited the sick, and catechized schoolchildren.

The novices pronounced their religious vows of holy poverty, chastity, and obedience in secret rites, since such Catholic promises were still formally outlawed in England; then the sixteen of them, who were now called scholastics, journeyed north to Stonyhurst College in Lancashire for one year of logic, epistemology, and mathematics, and two years of ethics and philosophy classes conducted solely in Latin, concentrating on the writings of Aristotle, Thomas Aquinas, and Francisco Suárez. And there Hopkins became preoccupied with the counterarguments of the thirteenth-century Franciscan philosopher Johannes Duns Scotus and his Oxford University commentaries on the *Sentences* of Peter Lombard.

Writing to Baillie, an Oxford classmate, of their Stonyhurst stints and privations, Hopkins noted with muted jealousy, "I hope you find yourself happy in town. This life here though it is hard is God's will for me as I most intimately know, which is more than violets knee-deep. This sprig of rhetoric brings me to a close. Believe me always your affectionate friend."

Concluding their Philosophate, the scholastics were assigned a work term called Regency that could last from one to five years. Capitalizing on his impressive diploma, the Province sent Hopkins back to Manresa House in Roehampton to teach rhetoric to the juniors—those scholastics who'd joined the Jesuits with an insufficiency of Latin and Greek or without university degrees. Considered a plum assignment in the British Province, it was for him a sort of long holiday outside London.

Hopkins was a marvel to his students—scholarly, amusing, incisive, pithy, and intolerant of shoddy reasoning—yet he worried that he taught stiffly and was reluctant to judge their papers and examinations for fear of falling into the established fault of critics: "to cramp and hedge in by rules the free movement of genius." So he was surprised but happy when his Regency was unexpectedly cut short in August 1874 and he was ordered to the Theologate of Saint Beuno's College in northern Wales for the studies necessary to receive ordination to the priesthood.

Soon after he arrived, he received tonsure and the four ancient, minor Orders of Doorkeeper, Reader, Exorcist, and

Acolyte, a preliminary to September 1877, when he would receive the Holy Orders of Subdeacon, Deacon, and Priest. In
high spirits, he wrote to his father about Saint Beuno's in his
first week there, noting:

> The house stands on a steep hillside and commands the long-
> drawn valley of the Clwyd to the Irish Sea, a vast prospect,
> and opposite is Mount Snowdon and its range, just now it be-
> ing bright visible but coming and going with the weather. The
> air seems to me very fresh and wholesome. Holidays till the
> 2nd of October. After that hours of very close study—lectures
> in dogmatic theology, moral ditto, canon law, church history,
> scripture, Hebrew and whatnot. I have half a mind to get up
> a little Welsh: all the neighbours speak it. I have said noth-
> ing about the house. It is built of limestone, decent outside,
> skimpin within, Gothic, like Lancing College done worse. The
> staircases, galleries, and bopeeps are inexpressible: it takes a
> fortnight to learn them. Pipes of affliction convey lukewarm
> water of affliction to some of the rooms, others more fortu-
> nate have fires. The garden is all heights, terraces, excelsiors,
> misty mountain tops, seats up trees called Crows' Nests,
> flights of steps seemingly up to heaven lined with burning as-
> piration upon aspiration of scarlet geraniums: it is very pretty
> and airy but it gives you the impression that if you took a step
> farther you would find yourself somewhere on Plenlimmon,
> Conway Castle, or Salisbury Craig.

In the first two years, the theology curriculum required
two hour-long lectures each morning, and on Mondays, Wed-
nesdays, and Fridays three additional lectures in the afternoon. Thursdays and Sundays were free, or *ad libitum*,

except for obligatory attendance at whatever liturgies were scheduled.

The seminarians woke at five-thirty and for an hour meditated on readings from the Holy Bible or on "points"— such as the giving of alms or the various kinds of humility— that were proposed by Rector James Jones on the previous night. Community Mass was at seven, but many of the priests said private Masses at side altars in the main chapel or in the Saint Agnes oratory, and each needed the assistance of an acolyte. Confessions were heard on Saturdays. Communion was usually received only on holy days of obligation and Sundays. A meager breakfast of oatmeal, jam, and toast was eaten at eight in silence, except for the announcements of the Beadle—or class secretary—and the reading of the great historical events or saints for that day in the *Roman Martyrology*. Just before the main dinner at one p.m., there was a silent examination of conscience in which the Jesuits sought to detect God's love, mercy, or correction in even the humdrum activities of the morning. Chosen scholastics read aloud hagiographies or books on spirituality as a form of dinner entertainment. Outdoor recreation or studies consumed the hours of the afternoon when there were no classes. Cakes and tea were served at five, and then there were "Circles" for practice in theological disputation. At seven-thirty there was a kind of lunch consisting of soup or meat pies or leftovers. Conversation in English was allowed then, though it was preceded by an extract from the "Menology," a calendar recording the heroism of those earlier English Roman Catholic religious who had endured execution, persecution, or exile since the age of Henry VIII.

On Monday evenings the seminarians discussed imaginary

sins and judicious counseling about them as preparation for hearing Confession. Each also practiced cadences and "tones" for effective sermon-giving. Otherwise there were card games, genial conversation, worldly reading, or billiards in the recreation rooms, though sometimes the three communities congregated for singing, playlets, or magic lantern shows. Litanies or a benediction service and another examination of conscience took place in the main chapel at nine p.m., and at ten the gaslights and candles were to be snuffed out.

Rules that would have been outrageous at any public school for boys were in great quantity at Saint Beuno's, where the men were mostly in their thirties. No theologian could visit another's room without permission, except for some practical matter such as filling an inkwell or getting a lucifer match, and even then the conversation would be limited to Latin. Walking to outlying villages was allowed, but generally only in groups of three that were called "companies." Mailed letters were routinely slit open as a sign that the Rector was entitled to read them if he wanted—he did not. Checking out a library book required the permission of Reverend Henry Edwards, the minister. Because there was just one eagle-clawed bathtub in the house, and an insufficiency of hot water, the residents of Saint Beuno's were restricted to one bath per week.

Looked at in a cynical way, the School of Theology was a prison of monotony and sustained uneventfulness, and more than once Hopkins delayed correspondence to his father or mother "in case anything should turn up, but nothing has." And yet Hopkins loved it there, loved the Welsh so much that he insisted "Hopkins" was a Celtic name, and even journals from his classmates record an unlikely joviality, enthusiasm, and earnestness in their vocation that is too frequently lacking in some softer ways of life. His friend Francis Bacon later wrote that he venerated Hopkins as a "saintly man" of great humility and unperturbed submission to the will of God. Joseph Rickaby's recollection was that Hopkins was "perhaps the most popular man in the house. Superiors and equals, everybody liked him. We laughed at him a good deal, but he took it good-humouredly, and joined in the amusement." And in his poem "In the Valley of the Elwy," Hopkins wrote of his happiness then:

I remember a house where all were good
  To me, God knows, deserving no such thing:
  Comforting smell breathed at very entering,
Fetched fresh, as I suppose, off some sweet wood.
That cordial air made those kind people a hood
  All over, as a bevy of eggs the mothering wing
  Will, or mild nights the new morsels of spring:
Why, it seemed of course; seemed of right it should.

•

Writing at a secretary in the scholastics' recreation room, he overheard Reverend Jones telling the Irishmen Kelly, Morrogh, and Gavin a joke about a Jesuit and a Dominican who smoked cigarettes as they read their breviaries outside together. The Dominican felt scruples about the propriety of that and thought they ought to consult their Superiors. When they next got together, he was surprised that the Jesuit was still smoking. The Jesuit asked how he'd framed the question to his Superior, and the Dominican said, "Am I permitted to smoke while I'm praying?" The Jesuit took another drag and said nothing. "Well, what did *you* say?" the Dominican asked. And the Jesuit answered, "Am I permitted to pray while I'm smoking?"

Enjoying the scholastics' laughter, the Rector left.

Cyprian Splaine finished reading *The Times* and strolled over to Hopkins. "Am I interrupting?"

Hopkins glanced up. "No, I'm at a loss."

Splaine glimpsed a title page of penciled handwriting that read:

THE WRECK OF THE DEUTSCHLAND
To the
happy memory of five Franciscan Nuns
exiles by the Falk Laws
drowned between midnight and morning of
Dec. 7th, 1875

"Are you writing a poem?"

Hopkins smiled. "Aren't you the clever one." He handed Splaine one of his interior pages.

Into the snow she sweeps,
   Hurling the haven behind,
The Deutschland, on Sunday; and so the sky keeps,
   For the infinite air is unkind,
And the sea flint-flake, black-backed in the regular blow,
Sitting Eastnortheast, in cursed quarter, the wind;
   Wiry and white-fiery and whirlwind-swivelled snow
Spins to the widow-making unchilding unfathering deeps.

Splaine could summon up only a confused "Interesting."

"You hate it."

Splaine scowled at the stanza again. "Are you sure of your meter, Gerard?"

"I call it 'sprung rhythm.' You scan it by accents or stresses alone, without counting the number of syllables. So a foot may be one strong syllable or it may be many light and one strong."

"An innovation of yours?"

"Actually not. We hear hints of it in popular jingles and nursery rhymes, such as '*Díng, dóng, béll; / Pússy's ín* the *wéll; Whó pút* her *ín? Líttle Jóhnny Thín. Whó púlled* her *óut? Líttle Jóhnny Stóut.*' So, too, '*One, twó, búckle* my *shóe.*'"

Without self-pity, Splaine admitted, "Well, I'm no poet."

Smiling as he took the page from him, Hopkins seemed happy to have disappointed. "Oh, it's a wreck this 'Wreck.' My rhymes carry over from one line into another, and there's a peculiar chiming inspired by Welsh poetry, and a great many more oddnesses that cannot but dismay an editor's eye. I shan't publish it. The journals will think it barbarous."

Splaine asked, "Why write it, then?"

In puzzlement Hopkins replied, "Why *pray*?"

•

His initial plan was simply to create a sea-disaster poem in his own strange, perplexing, passionate version of a Pindaric ode, and within weeks he'd written six eight-line stanzas of narrative on the shipwreck. But then he stalled. And why that was so became the subject of his prayer.

Hopkins was a child of a century in which many writers,

artists, and intellectuals abandoned not only Christianity but belief in God altogether. Their antipathies were generating a cultural shift away from organized religion and toward a view of God as only an interesting uncertainty. Whereas Hopkins considered God, as he wrote a friend, "an incomprehensible certainty." His was a faith that found hope and sturdiness even in the face of mystery, paradox, and philosophical difficulties. Because he'd felt God's love and tenderness so often in the past, he knew there was no meanness in him. There was justice, yes, and authority, and an awesome power that was greater than weather, greater than worlds. But usually there was just airy mystery, and on the bleakest occasions a sense of God watching with slack interest but resisting any temptation to intercede.

Hopkins recalled a dreary week in March during his second year of philosophy at Stonyhurst when he had received a letter from Henry Challis, an Oxford classmate and joint convert to Catholicism, now practicing as a barrister, saying he was giving up on the Church and religion altogether. And Hopkins was surprised by the hole it put in his heart. Challis and he were close friends at the Birmingham oratory, learning to teach in spite of classroom riot and jeering, commiserating with each other as they oversaw their houses of yelling, roistering, tameless schoolboys, and one night a week getting together in Hopkins's shabby suite for "séances," in which they shared stories about their dunces and scholars, the havoc in the dormitories, the latest hearsay out of London. Challis always supplied the port wine or sherry, "for I am the chalice and you the host." They speculated on the possible outcomes of controversies in the news, though Hopkins owned that "I live in bat-light and only shoot at a venture." But they were theologically in tune, and grateful for the acknowledging sympathy of a fellow convert whenever they tripped into some lapse or confusion that hereditary Catholics softly waltzed around.

Stricken by Challis's apostasy during his philosophy studies, Hopkins would write that he "was quite downcast: nature in all her parcels and faculties gaped and fell apart, like a clod cleaving and holding only by strings of root." He sat moonily at a Stonyhurst refectory table, squeezed between larger Jesuit scholastics, and with greater irritation seemed to notice the sloppiness of the opinions, the contentment with worn nostrums, the way some jolly dullards lunched upon an annual jest, and thrived and too long bloomed on it without other sustenance. In his vanity, the twenty-eight-year-old philosopher heard Jowett calling him "the star of Balliol," and he became the prey of fantasies of a London life without restrictions, in salons where the gaslights did not gutter out, where one chose one's own company, chose which of the world's library of books to read and how the hurly-burly of night would be spent. It was a time of such fruitless trial and stress that he'd wondered if he should quit the Society of Jesus. In one night prayer he'd asked, *Dear God, do you want us to fail?* But the *Lectio* at the next afternoon's dinner was a history of the seventeenth-century Frenchman Armand-Jean de Rancé, a womanizing priest of great wealth who was so struck by a Psalm insisting on submission and trust in the Lord that he was finally converted to a holy life, gave away his many possessions, and humbly entered the Cistercian abbey of La Trappe, which he'd inherited as a boy. Hopkins noted in his journal of March 13th, 1872, that when he heard that account "the mercy of God came strongly home to me too, so that I was choked for a little while and could not keep in my tears."

And in one morning prayer at Saint Beuno's, he recalled his Novitiate and his silent, thirty-day retreat with the *Spiritual Exercises* of Saint Ignatius. In the first week there was a meditation on sin in which the exercitant was asked to note God's attributes and their contraries in himself: to contrast God's wisdom with his own callowness, God's power with his frailty, God's justice with his iniquities, God's goodness with his wickedness, and to cry in wonder that he had been sustained, tolerated, and cared for in spite of his continuing insults and offenses.

Each of his memories of particular sins was like the penance of a schoolmaster's lashed rod, and as Hopkins walked into the Novitiate chapel after midnight his legs buckled, so that he fell into a kneel on the cold marble, and facing the tabernacle in his helplessness, he confessed his liabilities and wretchedness. He wept like a child and was glad for his isolation in the night silence of the wee hours. A human judge who viewed his soul would have condemned him, he thought; exacted some penalty; spurned him. But he felt in the presence of the Blessed Sacrament a tranquil, soothing God of intimacy and tolerance and unquenchable love, who knew to each jot and tittle everything about him but chose to focus on what was good, even childhood kindnesses that he'd forgotten. And then Hopkins said yes to whatever Christ would next ask of him, and grace as soft as a dove's wing floated over him, calming him, and he felt as steadied, poised, and paned as water in a well.

Without giving up on the stanzas he'd completed, Hopkins went up to his room in The Mansions one night and began his poem again, writing ten introductory stanzas of autobiography and homage to the Trinity: God who is "lightning and love" and "Father and fondler of heart thou hast wrung." With a pun on "mastering" as owning and controlling skills or talents but also captaining a ship, Hopkins initiated "Part the First" of "The Wreck of the Deutschland" with these stanzas:

1

Thou mastering me
God! giver of breath and bread;
World's strand, sway of the sea;
Lord of living and dead;
Thou hast bound bones and veins in me, fastened me flesh,
And after it almost unmade, what with dread,
Thy doing: and dost thou touch me afresh?
Over again I feel thy finger and find thee.

2

I did say yes
O at lightning and lashed rod;
Thou heardst me truer than tongue confess
Thy terror, O Christ, O God;
Thou knowest the walls, altar and hour and night:
The swoon of a heart that the sweep and the hurl of thee trod
Hard down with a horror of height:
And the midriff astrain with leaning of, laced with fire of stress.

4

THE PREY OF THE GALES

At five in the morning on Sunday, December 5th, Sister Henrica crouched into hot bathwater, acclimating to the burn and then sinking backward and holding her nose as she fully immersed. She felt skeins of hair folding over her face and floating aside, and she savored the excruciation of scalding before she rose again. A garden of steam bloomed in the cold, candlelit air of the ladies' bathing room. Wavelets rocked across the surface of the bath whenever the ship swerved at its anchor in the high winds. She held a bar of soap to her nose, deeply inhaling the hedonism of its lilac scent, and she washed slowly, with care, a slave to such luxury, until the water finally cooled. And then she got out, dried herself with the *Deutschland*'s fleecy Turkish towels, and hugged her woolen robe around her as she hustled barefoot down the corridor to her quarters.

She felt the ship's floor shift beneath her feet, and she gripped the lavatory stand as she stood naked in front of the hanging mirror. Cold was hardening her nipples as she considered a bath-flushed face that once meant to others Catharina. But who was now twenty-eight and still a virgin, and was gradually losing her prettiness to deprivation and lack of sleep. The cage of her ribs was too visible and her breasts, she thought, were becoming boyish. Wild as Medusa's the sorrel-brown hair she hid from the world. She would have Sister Brigitta cut it soon, but for now she hastily combed it back, twisted a handful into a chignon, and fixed it tight with hairpins.

The chimes of a brass chronometer tolled six times, and she went to the cabin wall and hit it twice with the flat of her hand. She called, "In Jesus Christ, my sisters, let us rise!"

And on the other side she heard the deep voice of Sister Barbara reply, "His glorious name be praised."

Sister Henrica rolled on knee-high black woolen stockings and tied the strings on a fresh cotton chemise and bloomers. She covered them with a flannel slip for more warmth and took out a chocolate-brown habit that hung in the closet. She forced her arms through its sleeves and her head through its yoke and squirmed it over her chest and hips as she recited, "Clothe my soul, O Lord, with the nuptial robe of chastity, that pure and undefiled I may wear it before thy throne of judgment."

She felt another sway underfoot and looked out the porthole at a wide swale of moonless night and shifting weather. Charcoal-black waves reared and collided and raced away from the cold northeasterly gale like giant horses at a gallop. And the *Deutschland* veered at its starboard anchor as if herded by them.

Sister Barbara was noticing the weather, too, and she opened her porthole just long enough to determine if she could scent a forecast of snow. She did. She tied the white cord cincture at her habit's waist and tucked her ears and hair inside the hood of a white linen coif and wimple as she recited, "O my dear Lord Jesus Christ, who for my sake became obedient even unto death on the cross, grant me the true spirit of religious duty and surrender."

Sister Norberta was not used to sharing a room. Undressing last night, she'd told Sister Barbara in a fidgety way, "Don't you look." So now, as Sister Norberta used stickpins to hold in place her starched white headband, Sister Barbara focused on the azure arabesques of the wallpaper, and she was putting on her own headband as she heard Sister Norberta whispering their common prayer, "Be thou, O Lord, a seal upon my forehead that I may be counted among the number of those who seek the light of the Lamb."

The ship rolled like a hound in its sleep, and Sister Brigitta fell a little toward the closet as she watched the childish Sister Aurea sleep a while longer, a fist near her face as if she'd been sucking her thumb. Sister Brigitta pinned on the order's heart-shaped black veil and softly recited, "Place on my head, O Lord, the helmet of salvation. O immaculate heart of Mary, obtain for me purity of body and soul."

She then shook Sister Aurea's right shoulder, and Sister Aurea smiled. "Are we there yet?"

Sister Brigitta said nothing as she adjusted her habit and veil in the carnality of a mirror. The ship yawed again and she tilted off-balance.

"Are we moving?" Sister Aurea asked.

"Yes. But not forward."

"I like the way the ship rocks," Sister Aurea claimed. "It's like sleeping in a hammock."

Sister Brigitta flatly said, "Eleven more days of it." And then she reminded the twenty-three-year-old, "We are still in the Great Silence."

Sister Aurea fastened both hands to her mouth as she got up, and Sister Brigitta giggled.

The four Sisters filed into Sister Henrica's cabin at six-thirty for "The Little Office of the Blessed Virgin Mary," and their Superior was as confident as Mother Clara in guiding them in the recitation of the four Psalms of Matins and the three Advent lessons on the Mother of Jesus from the Gospel According to Luke.

At seven the Great Silence ended and the five filed out to the dining room, where waiters stood by sideboards that held urns of hot coffee, straw baskets of hard rolls, and orange marmalade, chocolate slices, and cream.

Because they were shunned by the half-dozen other diners there, they had the freedom of their own table, and Sister Brigitta took the opportunity to instruct Sisters Barbara, Norberta, and Aurea in English. She held up a *Löffel* and told them, "Spoon." She held up a *Gabel*: "Fork." And a *Messer* was called "knife."

"Please your spoon pass me," she said in English, and Sister Norberta did so.

She looked at Sister Aurea and said in English, "Sugar now I vood like."

Sister Aurea was lost as she scanned the table.

"*Zucker,*" Sister Brigitta said. And in English, "Sugar."

"Shoo-care," Sister Aurea said.

Sister Brigitta said in stiff English, "In Missouri it may happen that you vill be understoot."

And she seemed so lofty and schoolteacherly that the Sisters fell into wild laughter.

•

Captain Eduard Brickenstein was stolid in the gaslit pilot-house, his hands folded behind his back in the stance of admiralty, staring eastward at the sea brink, the horns of the shore, and the faint house lights of Wremen. Saying nothing. His feet felt the humming throb of idling steam engines underneath him.

First Officer August Lauenstein hunched over a North Sea chart at a standing desk as he plotted their course with a wooden ruler. His hands shook with tremors in his need of drink, so he decided not to try penciling notations just yet.

"Snow," the captain said.

Lauenstein saw whirling flakes fly into the window glass and lose themselves in the greening sea. "At least we'll get a push."

The captain saw cold seamen in woolen stocking caps stationed on the foredeck, finding half-shelter in the windbreak of lifeboats and staring westward in the tedious duty of watch, their gloved hands holding the railing for stability on the seesawing vessel, their heads ducked underneath the collars of their peacoats as swerving snow attached to them. The flurries hindered his visibility only beyond a mile, and sunrise, he thought, would aid him. The stern lifted high on a great wave and precipitously sank again. Soon half a hundred passengers would be seasick. The captain told his mate, "Ancient mariners named the northeast wind Argestes."

Lauenstein said nothing.

Captain Brickenstein turned. "Tell Officer Tramultz to weigh anchor."

"Aye aye," Lauenstein said.

•

The *Deutschland* steered a westerly course at a speed of twelve knots—close to fourteen miles per hour—and lost sight of land. And when the topsail on the foremast was hoisted, the ship gained a half-knot of speed. At noon the mate took a sounding with a rope and weighted bucket and found that twelve fathoms below them was a seafloor of fine sand, a good sign. At half-past one in the afternoon, Lauenstein recorded in the ship's log that the lightship off the spa island of Borkum was one mile to the port side as they steamed past, so they were perfectly on course. Since magnets could be affected by the great tonnage of iron on a ship, all five compasses were compared for accuracy, and only the slightest deviations were discovered. Then Captain Brickenstein himself took the helm for a while, steering a west-southwesterly course into air that was hazy with snowfall.

Earlier, around ten, Sister Barbara and Sister Norberta had hazarded a constitutional on the breezy belvedere of the weather deck, their veils swarming around their heads as they strolled toward the bow and yanking away from them like pennants as they tilted determinedly toward the stern. They could see no land, no other ship, just the rise and fall of a North Sea that was veined like green marble with the sliding white crests and striations of the swells. Wide curtains of snow hung from far-off castlings of dark gray cloud, and above them were the roiling white hills and towers of cumulus clouds that seemed huge as cities. But for the moment the only inclemency in their sea-lane was the cold and the wind and the salty mists that found them whenever an occasional rolling house of wave blasted against the windward hull and the water atomized.

The first-class passenger Carl Dietrich Meyer wore a long sable coat and hat as he huddled between two able seamen in order to light his meerschaum pipe. And then he straightened, puffing a sweet aromatic smoke that carried the scent of plums, and he watched the seamen use straw brooms to sweep the dusting of snow from the canvas tarpaulins that covered the lifeboats. Herr Meyer helpfully offered some instructions on improving their method, but the seamen seemed not to be listening. Seeing the strolling nuns, Meyer waved them over, sought their names, and introduced them to the seamen August de Vries and Eilert Schiller, and then, as the Sisters turned again toward the foredeck, he hastened to join them.

Whether he was lonely or merely loquacious was unclear, but he seemed to derive abundant pleasure in occupying Sisters Barbara and Norberta with his learning on the oceans. There was enough water in the four oceans and seventy seas, he said, for each person on earth to have one hundred billion gallons. There was enough sodium chloride in them to blanket all the continents in a salt overstory five hundred feet thick. Also strewn uselessly in the oceans was far more gold—nine million tons was the estimate—than had ever been mined on land. And there was the enormous power of the waves and tides to consider. Herr Meyer informed the two *Fräulein* that engineers in France measured instances in which waves hurled over a wall that was twenty feet high some breakwater boulders weighing seven thousand pounds, and the tallest wave on record was the one that hit Siberia's Kamchatka Peninsula in 1737, at a height of two hundred and ten feet above sea level. Almost the size of a twenty-story building. Imagine it!

Sister Norberta had forgotten about the male fascination with facts. With insincerity, she noted, "What interesting arithmetic."

Sister Barbara elbowed her.

Carl Dietrich Meyer seemed not to notice. Tamping his pipe tobacco with the head of a roofing nail, he told them,

"Well, I do count myself an intellectual as well as a business-man. Of course, an intellectual is what an overeducated man calls himself when he has no particular talents."

Sister Barbara charitably said, "But your talent for con-versation is much in evidence."

"Is it? I'm glad."

"I'm chilly," Sister Norberta said.

Herr Meyer smiled. "Oh well, hurry in, then! We shall have other opportunities to chat and dispute on this long voyage."

Crossing through the hatchway with Sister Barbara, Sis-ter Norberta risked the joke, "I have just had my vocation to chastity confirmed."

•

As she'd done as a shopgirl in Cologne, Sister Henrica spent the morning strolling the corridors of the *Deutschland* while reading a book, in this case *The Autobiography of Saint Ig-natius Loyola*, which she'd been given by Salzkotten's chap-lain because the sixteenth-century founder of the Society of Jesus generally referred to himself as a pilgrim, just as she was now. Writing of himself in the third person, Ignatius noted the first stirrings of a religious vocation as he healed from se-rious injuries after the French siege of the citadel of Pam-plona. She read:

> When he was thinking about the things of the world, he took
> much delight in them, but afterward, when he was tired and
> put them aside, he found that he was dry and discontented.
> But when he thought of going to Jerusalem, barefoot and eat-
> ing nothing but herbs and undergoing all the other rigors that
> he saw the saints had endured, not only was he consoled when

he had these thoughts, but even after putting them aside, he remained content and happy.

Sister Henrica thought, *Yes. Exactly.*

The *Deutschland* yawed with a sea shift, and she was flung hard into a wall, so she closed the book on a finger and gripped it against her waist as she continued a journey through the chaos and children's noise and Slavic languages of steerage until she arrived at a hatchway to the cargo hold.

There Quartermaster August Bock was kneeling between high stacks of freight and using a hammer to claw open a fallen wooden crate printed with the words STAATLICHE PORZELLAN-MANUFAKTUR MEISSEN.

When she was a little girl, she'd hoped for the birthday gift of a hand-painted figurine from the famous Meissen porcelain factory, so it pained her to see Quartermaster Bock fuming as he rummaged through the straw packing and laid aside like flotsam the delicate and heartbreakingly lovely doll's heads that had been shattered, cracked, or chipped in their fall from a high shelf.

She asked, "What are you going to do with them?"

She'd approached so softly that Bock glanced up in surprise. Then he inspected and rejected another. "Report them lost at sea," he said.

"Would you mind if I took some of them?"

The quartermaster fretted over it. "How many?"

She gave it some thought and said, "Four."

He shrugged.

And Sister Henrica inquired, "Where could I find glue?"

•

The five Sisters gathered in Sister Henrica's room to recite the so-called little hours of Prime, Terce, and Sext, then filed into the dining hall at 1:00 p.m. for a grand Sunday dinner that included Reinhold Haart's Riesling Piesporter wine. Then Sister Henrica joined Sister Barbara and Sister Norberta for a cold constitutional on the *Deutschland*'s weather deck. Crests of wave raveled up into the air in arching whips and straps of glassy spray until they were broken into clouds of white and blew away. Under each curl shone a bright juice of beautiful green. Sister Barbara asked Sister Henrica how she would describe that color, and she gave it thorough consideration before saying, "Chrysoprase."

Sister Norberta scowled. "What on earth is that?"

Sister Henrica gently told her, "A mineral used for gems. The green of leeks mixed with gold."

Sister Barbara stared out at the North Sea for a while before confirming, "She's right."

•

Sister Brigitta and Sister Aurea spent their liberty in the *Deutschland*'s library, leafing through popular romances that Mother Clara would have forbidden them, and regaling each other by reading aloud florid passages with fustian melodrama. Then an Englishman in a gray tweed suit wandered in and their naughtiness and giggling had to end.

He took out of his suitcoat pocket spectacles without frame or skull temples that he carefully pinched onto the bridge of his nose, and when he saw Sister Aurea gaping, Charles Dore Harvey, who would outlast the ordeal, told her in German they were a new invention called pince-nez. And then he introduced himself as the Thames River pilot to whom North German Lloyd gave free room and board and a week's wages for his few hours of expertise.

"It must be nice being you," Sister Aurea said.

"Or one could just as easily say, 'I have climbed to the top of the greasy pole.'" Seeing Sister Aurea's puzzlement, he explained, "It's what Benjamin Disraeli said when he became Britain's Prime Minister."

Confused, she just stared.

With a vanity he disguised as amazement, Harvey told them in ungrammatical German that this was his one-hundred-twenty-first voyage across the North Sea, and he harried them with stories of his sterling Navy career as he unfolded a nautical chart on the library table to indicate the sea-lane from Bremerhaven to Harwich. The Sisters tipped off-balance as the ship wallowed with a surge of wave, but the English Channel pilot's shoes were widely planted and he seemed not to notice the seesawing that was whitening Sister Aurea's face. He estimated they were now twenty miles north of the chain of the West Frisian Islands, which belonged to the Netherlands. Were he a gambling man, he'd bet a shilling they were now on the longitude of the island named Ameland and would be off the coast of Terschelling Island by four.

"I feel ill," Sister Aurea said, and she fraily sat on the library's satin Empire Méridienne sofa.

Harvey ignored the girl as he told Sister Brigitta that the West Germanic Frisian language was the one most closely related to English, and on his first visit to Terschelling, oh, thirty years ago, he discovered he could converse quite well with the innkeeper even though Harvey did not then *spreche Deutsch.*

Sister Brigitta worriedly asked her friend, "Are you all right?"

Sister Aurea woozily stood, sustained some seconds of introspection, then hurried out of the library with a hand held to her mouth.

Charles Dore Harvey calmly watched as she exited, took off his pince-nez to clean the lenses with his handkerchief, and then smiled at Sister Brigitta as he quoted in English, " 'Seasickness is the inarticulate expression of pain we feel on seeing a proselyte escape us just as we were on the point of capturing it.' " She had no reaction, so he carved quotes with his fingers as he credited the author: "Samuel Butler."

Sister Brigitta understood nothing of his English, and she was relieved to tell him in German, "I have to go see how she is."

"Naturally," he said in German, and began folding up the nautical chart. "Cheerio."

•

At four in the afternoon, some eighteen miles off the coast of Terschelling, Second Officer Carl Thalenhorst hunched outside into a colder northeasterly wind and lashing, nearly horizontal snow. When he got to the stern, he cast off a large triangle of balsa wood that was weighted so it would float upright and manifest itself to the ship. Attached to it like the string of a kite was a rope knotted at equal distances of fifty-one feet, so that one hundred twenty knots approximated a nautical mile. Watching the rope feed out, the second officer counted thirteen knots in thirty seconds, and hauled the line and its "log" back in. With such crude measurements and a compass reading their location could be calculated in the mathematical process called dead reckoning, but it was like situating oneself in a state, not a city. And with the skies clouded, the trigonometry of sextant and chronometer was impossible. Voyages in 1875 sometimes involved a ship simply blundering from one place to another.

Carl Thalenhorst headed back to the pilothouse, but the icy seawater had stiffened his hands so much he couldn't hold a pen, hence Captain Brickenstein himself recorded their speed at thirteen knots in the ship's log. And he contributed the terse note, "Thick weather."

The squalls of snow continued with nightfall, and the unpredictable rolling and lurching of the *Deutschland* caused many seasick passengers to skip the light evening meal—an *Eintopf*, or stew, of potatoes, beans, peas, carrots, sausage, and spices. Sisters Aurea and Norberta were confined to their cabins and Sister Barbara volunteered to nurse them, so only Sisters Henrica and Brigitta ventured into a grand saloon paneled with bird's-eye maple and buttressed by oak pilasters inlaid with rosewood, and with leafy, gilt capitals. Hanging between brass gaslights were eight oil paintings by Franz Hünten, each a mediocre seascape of shipping and fishing vessels in full sail. Empire sofas and thirty armchairs were matched with Biedermeier tables and hand-painted cabinets and sideboards that held samovars of coffee and tea. Three tinkling chandeliers swayed with the sea.

Sister Brigitta got saucers and teacups and filled them from the urns as Sister Henrica sat stiffly upright on a loveseat. She watched hissing snow seethe against the mullions of the twelve windowpanes of the skylight but melt with the radiator heat and streak away like rain. Charles Dore Harvey entered the saloon, examined its population, waved a fond hello to Sister Brigitta, and withdrew. A mother was reading to a child as a shawled infant slept in the width of her lap. The Russian named Papolkoff had wedged his hands and a snifter of Cognac between his thighs. His head fell forward; he jerked awake; his head fell forward again. Three men in suits and cravats huddled in earnest financial conversation. Chess players considered their pieces on the board. Some older women were muttering about their health. A husband tilted toward his wife and whispered something as he sneered at the nuns.

Sister Brigitta said, "This is Heymann Nathan," and Sister Henrica turned.

Carrying their saucers and steaming teacups was a tall, lean, handsome man in his thirties with a full black beard and a Jewish skullcap pinned to the wild, helical nest of his hair. Setting their saucers and teacups on the Biedermeier table at their knees, he asked in a slightly accented German if he could join them.

Nathan dragged over a dining chair and straddled it as she had seen only Americans do, folding his arms across its crown as he displayed his plumage, saying he was born in Hamburg but as a boy emigrated to New York City, where he attended a Brooklyn high school and now managed a jewelry store on Maiden Lane. He was not yet married; hoped to be someday. Mother would be so pleased. Completing a diamond-buying trip to Antwerp, he had decided to visit grandparents in northern Germany, and now he was heading back for the important holiday sales. Nathan learned the Sisters spoke some English and he relaxed into that. "So, you two," he said. "No husbands?"

"We do not marry," Sister Henrica said.

"Oh, that's right. Excuse me. What a nincompoop."

"To Missouri vee go, vee fife nuns," Sister Brigitta tried in English, and she was surprised and pleased when he understood.

"I was there once. Saint Louis."

"Vee alzo to Sankt Louis are going!"

"Carondelet," Sister Henrica said.

Nathan faced gorgeous Sister Brigitta. "There's a bird there, a meadowlark? You hear it in the fields in the morning. They say its song is 'Pretty girl, wake up!' "

Sister Brigitta was lost, so Sister Henrica translated for her. Sister Brigitta pinked as she sipped her tea.

"Like this," Nathan said, and whistled his imitation of a country meadowlark.

The nuns fell into laughter, shyly holding their hands up to hide their teeth.

"But what do I know from rural life?" he said. "I'm a city boy."

"In New York City, vee haff just one day," Sister Henrica said.

Nathan nodded. A silence descended and the Sisters' difficulties with English held the curtain down. The Sisters delicately sipped their tea as criticism sought the three from various parts of the grand saloon.

"Well," Heymann Nathan sighed, and unstraddled his chair and urged them in German to sleep well. And as he headed out, he cocked a thumb toward the saloon's occupants and said in English, "Don't let the goyim get to you."

The stewardess Catharina Schlossbauer walked up in a white-aproned maid's dress and tipped forward pettishly, her hands on her knees, as she asked if the *Schwestern* wished some chocolate torte.

"Shall we go?" Sister Henrica asked the younger nun.

Sister Brigitta fitted her teacup in its saucer. "Everything was very nice," she told the stewardess, but she'd already turned to another group.

Walking to their cabins, the Sisters gaily sang in duet Jacques Offenbach's *Barcarolle,* the song of the Venetian gondoliers.

•

Writing his mother from Saint Beuno's on the 26th of June 1876, Hopkins noted:

You ask about my poem on the Deutschland. You forget that we have a magazine of our own, *The Month.* I have asked Fr. Coleridge the editor, who is besides my oldest friend in the Society, to take it, but I had to tell him that I felt sure he wd. personally dislike it very much, only that he was to consider not his tastes but those of *The Month*'s readers. He replied that there was in America a new sort of poetry which did not rhyme or scan or construe; if mine rhymed and scanned and construed and did not make nonsense or bad morality he did not see why it shd. not do. So I sent it. Hitherto he has not answered; which is a sign it cannot appear in the July number but otherwise seems to shew he means to take it.

28 June

I have heard from him this morning. The poem was too late for July but will appear in the August number. He wants me however to do away with the accents which mark the scanning. I would gladly have done without them if I had thought my readers would scan right unaided but I am afraid they will not, and if the lines are not rightly scanned they are ruined.

Still I am afraid I must humour an editor, but some lines at all
events will have to be marked.

You must never say that the poem is mine.

With best love to all I am your loving son,

GERARD M. HOPKINS, S.J.

•

On July 28th, 1876—Hopkins's thirty-second birthday—
Reverend Doctor James Brown visited the Jesuits of Saint
Beuno's to celebrate his twenty-fifth anniversary as an ecclesiastic and to join in their founder's day feast for Saint Ignatius Loyola on July 31st. Brown, the Bishop of Shrewsbury,
had been installed as a prelate soon after the Roman Catholic
episcopal hierarchy finally was restored in England after
three centuries of persecution. Rector James Jones requested
that Hopkins write poems in honor of the bishop in English,
Latin, and Welsh, to be joined with Reverend John Morris's
sermon and other writings commemorating the anniversary,
and a handsome album was printed that contained "The Silver Jubilee" in English, *"Ad Episcopum Salopiensem"* in
Latin, and *"Cywydd"* in Welsh, each attributed to a humble
G.M.H.

They were the only original poems by Hopkins that he
would ever see published as a Jesuit, for on August 6th he was
writing his father that "The Wreck of the Deutschland" was
not, after all, in the August *Month*, and whether it would be in
the September number or in any he could not yet learn. Altogether, he noted, it had cost him a good deal of consternation.

On September 23rd, he wrote to his mother, "About
the Deutschland 'sigh no more,' I am glad now it has not
appeared."

Reverend Henry Coleridge was a former Fellow at Oriel College at Oxford and the initial publisher of John Henry Newman's dramatic poem "The Dream of Gerontius," and yet he seemed to have had misgivings about his own poetic judgment, and the queerness of "The Wreck of the Deutschland" caused him to ask a subeditor at *The Month* for a second opinion on the poem by the pseudonymous "Crow of Maenefa." The subeditor's opinion was that the thirty-five esoteric stanzas were hardly readable and had only managed to give him a headache. And so the handwritten pages were eventually returned to Hopkins with regrets.

Recalling the *Spiritual Exercises* of Saint Ignatius Loyola, Hopkins accepted the recommendation that he "should not prefer health to sickness, riches to poverty, honor to dishonor, a long life to a short life," but choose "what is more conducive to the end for which we are created," which was "to praise, reverence, and serve God our Lord." Whether he published his poetry or not seemed to the conscientious Hopkins another vagary over which a good Jesuit should exercise no partiality. And so at some cost to his vanity and notions of excellence in the arts, he quieted his irritation with *The Month* by shifting his attention to his studies.

In the wrought-iron roost in the dining hall, he preached a practice Sunday sermon—called a "Dominical"—on the gospel reading from John on the feeding of the five thousand. But his reputation for mischief was such that his congregation of friends thought his fussy solemnities hilarious and he was forced to end his sermon a full page short of its conclusion. Also, as a senior member of the Saint Beuno's debating club, he spoke for the proposition, which carried, "that every scholastic should have assigned to him from the end of his noviceship some branch of study in which he could labour to excel" and "that the modern system of education is not suited to promote the highest mental development," which also carried the vote.

But the full days were fatiguing. Writing to his mother on her birthday, March 3rd, 1877, he explained that his third-year class was to be examined in moral theology to see whether they were fit to hear confessions and correctly counsel sinners. "Going over moral theology over and over again and in a hurry is the most wearisome work and tonight at all events I am so tired I am good for nothing. But by Saturday night this will be over." Noting the weather—"very sharp frost with bitter north winds"—venting annoyance at having missed the eclipse of the moon, and reporting that "we have primroses about us," Hopkins also sent along "two sonnets I wrote in a freak the other day; they will make a little birthday gift. They are not so very queer, but have a few metrical effects, mostly after Milton."

Those sonnets were "The Starlight Night" and "God's Grandeur," and in the next months of 1877 he would produce "The Sea and the Skylark," "The Windhover," "Pied Beauty," and "Hurrahing in Harvest," a clutch of poems that were so original and are now so esteemed that 1877 has since been considered his *annus mirabilis*, Hopkins's miracle year.

Rickaby once paused at his door on his way downstairs to say it was time for dinner.

"Right there."

Rickaby asked, "Why are you so happy?"

Hopkins got up from his desk and quoted William Wordsworth on poetry: "Oh, it's just the spontaneous overflow of powerful feelings."

"That old thing," Rickaby said.

But there were spells even then of cheerlessness, dank exhaustion, insomnia, and dark tempests of the mind whose
cause, he thought, was his nagging studies. With each suc-
ceeding year, however, the malady would be a greater affliction, and he would remember the Hell of John Milton's
Paradise Lost, where there was "No light, but rather dark-
ness visible" and "Regions of sorrow, doleful shades, where
peace / And rest can never dwell, hope never comes . . ."

•

With the onset of night on December 5th, 1875, Captain Eduard Brickenstein had wisely steered toward the deeper middle channel of the North Sea in order to avoid the hazardous
shoals of the Dutch coast. Winds of gale force were shoving
them westward, and when the captain estimated the ship to
be off the heights of west Terschelling Island, he ordered
the helmsman onto a more southerly heading to correct their
drift. With the squalling snow and the moonless, starless
night, Captain Brickenstein was navigationally blind and just
guessing about their location, and though he thought the
Deutschland was steaming southward toward the seaside re-
sort of Margate and the twenty-mile-wide Strait of Dover
that connected the North Sea with the English Channel, the
ship was instead on a diagonal course for the sandbanks that
were like great bones beneath the skin of the sea in the
Thames River estuary.

Around eleven, the energetic and extroverted Carl Dietrich Meyer visited the pilothouse in his long sable coat. Wide
awake, he said, because he'd had too much coffee. Captain
Brickenstein was still up, overseeing the helmsman, and was

too new to his job on the *Deutschland* to be impatient with a first-class passenger. Herr Meyer was shown the heading on the compass and was permitted some exhilarating minutes at the helm. His hands whitened with the urgency of the task, but his huge smile was square and big-toothed and boyish.

The helmsman took over again, and Captain Brickenstein took Herr Meyer to the chart, illustrating their course by sliding his forefinger along a sea-lane that paralleled the Suffolk coastline in the surety halfway between the Galloper and North Hinder sandbanks, the distance between them being twelve and a half miles.

With the joy and conceit of a man who was both highly educated and rich, Carl Dietrich Meyer conveyed his nautical information about their treacherous route. Wasn't it in the great storm of September 1671 that seventy-five ships were wrecked off the east coast of England? And as recently as October 1820, if his history was correct, and he felt sure it was, there were five shipwrecks in just one month on the sandbanks off Harwich. Weekly events!

Captain Brickenstein glowered. "But none from North German Lloyd's fleet."

Carl Dietrich Meyer grinned. "Oh, but I have nipped up against a seafarer's superstition, haven't I? I shall unsay all I have said. No troubles, no danger, smooth sailing for us. Are we properly unhexed now?"

Captain Brickenstein gruffly faced away from him, and Carl Dietrich Meyer announced he was going to bed, later recalling that the o'clock was eleven-thirty.

•

At two a.m. on Monday, December 6th, they were still running at thirteen and one-half knots, or slightly more than fifteen miles per hour, and seemed to be on course. The captain ordered the steam engines idled and hove to in order to have the sand bottom sounded. Brickenstein was told the depth was twenty-one fathoms, or one hundred twenty-six feet. But the seafloor shifted like dunes in an Egyptian wind, so just because the chart called for a depth of seventeen fathoms, he was not skeptical about their direction or locale.

At three in the morning, the captain hove to again, yanked on a woolen stocking cap, and went out with Able Seaman Heinz Forsenstein, holding his officer's black peacoat collar tight at his throat in the smarting snow and cold of the night as he closely watched the seaman take another sounding. The captain was surprised by a report of twenty-five fathoms—it ought to have been nineteen—but pleased that the weighted bucket scraped up only fine sand and none of the scourings and remnants of surf. He went down to the galley for coffee.

At four in the morning, Siegfried Benning, the ship's purser, who was on watch, awoke Charles Dore Harvey to say they seemed to be nearing the eastern approaches to the mouth of the Thames River. Harvey would be at the helm of the *Deutschland* through the Solent—the channel between the Isle of Wight and the mainland of southern England—and steer the ship up Southampton Water. He joined Lauenstein on the weather deck for another sounding that detected a depth of only seventeen and a half fathoms, and the sand still fine. But the winds were ever more fierce. Employing the scale invented by Sir Francis Beaufort, Harvey determined that the astern storm was a Force 10, described as a "whole gale" of fifty-five to sixty-three miles per hour. At seventy-five miles per hour they would be in a hurricane. Consequently, Captain Brickenstein had the fore-topsail taken in and wrapped, and he telegraphed First Engineer Reinhold Schmidt below to have the engines run at half-speed. Even at that, the *Deutschland* was surging toward the perilous east coast of England at nine and one-half knots.

Consulting sea charts for the course he guessed he was on, the captain saw no numbers that corresponded to the soundings that had been made through the night. And he realized he had not taken into account the direction and set of the tide, which was with them almost all the way. A helmsman steering wrongly by only a hairsbreadth—one forty-eighth of a degree—would find his ship one-third of a mile off its intended course after a hundred miles, and with the skewing snowstorm and a pitch-black night, even noting such nautical errors was out of the question. The *Deutschland* was in fact thirty miles from where Brickenstein thought it ought to be, a full hour ahead of his estimations and some eighteen miles to the west, and heading with velocity for the very sandbanks he'd sought to avoid.

Eilert Schiller was one of six seamen serving as lookouts on the weather deck, though the storm conditions limited their vision to the point of uselessness. Just before five, Schiller noticed to the port side a flash of light, then another flash, as on a warning buoy, but when he reported what he'd seen, Captain Brickenstein presumed it was the beacon at the North Hinder sandbank, whose fixed beam could have been interrupted by swells and clouds of snow. Soon he would realize it was the flashing warning beacon of the lightship anchored near the sandbank called the Kentish Knock— "*Knock*" being a Celtic word for hill.

August Lauenstein reported for duty, discerned the captain's mystification about their position, and took his own sounding of seventeen fathoms. Seaman Forsenstein held a coal-oil lantern over the bucket as Lauenstein examined its contents and lifted a handful. "Sand," he said. "And mussel shells."

"Oh no," the seaman said.

Lauenstein ran to the pilothouse with the news. And just then Captain Brickenstein noted the white horseheads of surf that indicated the underwater island of a sandbank, and he immediately telegraphed the engine room, "Stop and full speed astern."

Reinhold Schmidt promptly reversed the engines and studied the ship's exertions against a strong current, rising and settling with each high swell, until there was a jolt against some hidden geology. Schmidt was shocked by a loud, clanking sound and noticed the dual engines racing as the driveshaft spun without resistance. The lone screw propeller had sheared off while digging into the seafloor.

The captain, his mate, the English Channel pilot, and the helmsman felt the *Deutschland* drifting after the first jolt and braced themselves against the pilothouse walls or held on to the bolted chart table for the impact that they felt sure was soon to come.

·

Because December 6th was the gifting feast of Saint Nicholas, Sister Henrica was sneaking into the Sisters' quarters and depositing ribboned red tissue bags of hazelnuts and candies in each right shoe and a Meissen porcelain doll repaired with glue in each left. She'd just finished the secret deliveries when she was jounced against a doorframe with the ship's first jolt, and she was in the corridor when she heard a mysterious scraping, screaming noise of the keel riding an underwater sand dune. And then there was a sudden, crunching, hull-booming halt to their motion that hurled her onto her hands and knees, skidded cutlery, dishware, and urns onto the dining-room floor, and tossed the wakened passengers in steerage like jacks.

The incoming tide was at its highest level, and it slewed the ship around so that its port side was eastward and tipped down. Heavy, detonating sea swells crashed broadside into the run-aground *Deutschland*, flooding into the sizzling stoke-hold so that all the gaslights were extinguished, the hot glass water gauges burst, and a swamp of steam scalded Schmidt and his stokers until they rushed out into the howling storm of the weather deck. And there a swell broke across the ship, spilling a stoker who would have been lost at sea had his shoe not caught in a scupper.

The night, the snow, and the vast cloud of steam that rose up from the ship made it impossible for Captain Brickenstein to see even as far as the giant funnel, and he was tortured by the certainty that already some of his crew were overboard out there in the tyranny of the sea, vainly waving their arms for a rescue that would not come in time, their voices raised in stricken calls that could not be heard.

A great wave the very size of the *Deutschland* struck it in the full blast of a hundred tons, slamming it almost onto its side, and the shock upended Quartermaster August Bock, who slid helplessly on his back on the deck until he banged hard into the pilothouse, where Lauenstein reached out to haul him inside. Winded after his brush with sure death, Bock could only manage, "Lifeboats?"

"The cannon first," Captain Brickenstein said.

Confusion was general below, especially in steerage, where there was now three inches of water and no lights. Even in second and first class all the corridors and stairways were filled with crying passengers, most still in their nightclothes and robes, some shrieking with each crash of a wave as they worried that the iron sides and stays of the *Deutschland* were being torn from their rivets by the sea.

Crew members were sidling through the crowd distributing cork life vests and announcing a probable disembarkation when the five Sisters exited from their cabins in their full habits and cloaks and mittens. Huddling around their Superior, some wept and prayed the Rosary as they strapped on their life vests, but little Sister Aurea cradled the hand-painted porcelain doll in her arms, mothering it as she smiled and said, "I love my gift, Sister."

Sister Henrica could not smile back. "I hoped you would."

Sister Barbara was helping Sister Brigitta with the straps as she said, "And so exactly in the spirit of Saint Nicholas. Our children in the hospital will love them."

Sister Aurea asked, "And it's Mother Clara's birthday, too, isn't it?"

"Yes."

"Would she have heard about the dolls?"

"No."

Sister Aurea was astonishing. "She'll be how old today?"

There was a cracking noise from a great wave and then the enormous thunder of a jolt that shoved the crowd against each other. Sister Aurea was still waiting for an answer and Sister Henrica tried to recall. "She'll be forty-eight."

"I'm naming my doll Clara. Won't Mother be pleased?"

Sister Norberta was scowling at the girl, and she started to scold, "Have you any idea—"

But Sister Henrica touched a shushing finger to her lips. Sister Norberta obediently turned away.

"I'm hungry," Sister Aurea said.

In the pilothouse, Charles Dore Harvey was examining the North Sea charts as August Lauenstein read aloud the ship's log of soundings, until the English Channel pilot determined that the *Deutschland* was thirty miles offshore on the six-and-a-half-mile-long sandbank called the Kentish Knock, southeast of Harwich and due north of Margate, and twenty miles from the English coast, next to Galloper the outermost shoal at the mouth of the Thames, and at low tide only a fathom deep.

Lauenstein reported their reckoning as the captain watched seething waves wash over the stuck-fast ship fore and aft. With cool irritation the captain stated, "Too little too late, is it not?"

Waves twice crashed Reinhold Schmidt and a seaman clear across the ship's stern before they could roll out the infantry cannon that would announce the jeopardy of their situation to rescue boats or other passing ships, since the ship-to-shore telegraph had not yet been invented. But the flash vent in the cannon was jammed, and in using a screwdriver and ball-peen hammer to wedge and jar the vent open, Schmidt let salt water in and saturated the gunpowder.

Seeing Schmidt droop his head in dejection, Brickenstein cursed with disgust and instructed Lauenstein to blow the steam whistle, then ordered August Bock and Otto Tramultz to lower the lifeboats.

There were four on each side of the ship, hanging from cranelike devices called davits. Otto Tramultz and four seamen jumped into Boat #1 as the winches unreeled, intending to hold the vessel steady with oars and boat hooks so the first two shivering women and their crying children could board. But a swell rushed the seventy-passenger iron lifeboat hard up against the *Deutschland*, and in overrocking backward, Boat #1 filled almost to its gunwales with water, adding such great weight that the three-inch-thick rope painter on its bow snapped with the strain and a swell carried the iron lifeboat off into the night, still sinking.

The last thing Captain Brickenstein witnessed of Otto Tramultz was the Arctic explorer standing tall on the sailing thwart and waving one hand, not for rescue but in a slow farewell.

Second Officer Carl Thalenhorst and Dietrich Stege, the ship's carpenter, were still at the winches of Boat #4 when a giant breaker smashed it against the *Deutschland* so that its hull was stove inward and rent at its seams, and the surf skidded the two men across the width of the ship until the starboard railing saved them.

Quartermaster Bock and Seaman Forsenstein were in Boat #3, tugging the tarpaulin cover off a seventy-passenger wooden cutter, or sloop, with double-banked oars. A passenger whose name was unknown to the quartermaster loped across the deck in order to jump in with them. But just then a wave fell into the lifeboat like a building, tearing it from its davits, and upending it and the three men into the cold sea. As the three men thrashed up to the surface, gasping for air, another sea swell miraculously rolled the sloop over so that Bock could get his left leg over the gunwale and struggle aboard. Forsenstein was at the sloop's bow, shinnying onto a painter still stiff with ice and holding the coughing passenger by the collar of his mackinaw coat. Currents were carrying them away from the ship as Bock got the other two into the sloop. The nameless passenger's skull was cracked and blood bootlaced his face as he tottered forward and huddled like a child in the prow of the sloshing boat.

Watching from the pilothouse, Brickenstein could see Bock and Forsenstein slam oars in the oarlocks and try to row the sloop back toward the *Deutschland*, but the sea was too strong and the boat too heavy, and a swift-running swell carried their sloop off into the night, their speed down the wave's face like that of a toboggan on a steep slope. And then there was nothing of them to see.

August Bock. Whose wife feared just this. *She believes we are going to have an unlucky time of it.*

In spite of the howling storm, more passengers were rushing out to the iron lifeboats with hopes of escape, then scurrying in retreat from the cannon noise and icy spray of wave explosions that were as high and wide as white oak trees. The sea in its fury yanked another iron boat off its davits as Brickenstein went outside, held an American megaphone to his mouth, and shouted, "Stop with the lifeboats! The sea won't let us!"

The crew immediately ran back inside the hatchways, and the stunned passengers hurried after them.

Chief Engineer Reinhold Schmidt went down to the gymnasium of the engine room as to his home and found it still flooding, his journal and pencils and machine manuals rocking and circling on the rising water. But he was able to convert the ship's three steam spray pumps into suction hoses and passed out five hand pumps to the crew so that steerage could at least be maintained at wading depth.

Second Officer Carl Thalenhorst shot a rocket overhead just before sunrise and marveled as it burst redly in the heavens "like the loveliest of Holland tulips." Eighteen rockets in all were fired between six in the morning and nine, each seen by the three-man crew on the Kentish Knock lightship three miles away. But anchored, with neither steam power nor sail, and with no wireless communications, the crew on the Knock lightship could do no more than respond with cannon shots that were answered by the crew of the Sunk lightship but not heard by anyone on the *Deutschland*.

Remarkably, breakfast was served—hot buns and coffee, hard-boiled eggs, and three varieties of cheese—and though some passengers ate in the dining room with their coats and gloves and cork life vests still on, the general feeling was that of inconvenience and a calm, cautious waiting for rescue, an optimism inspired by the stewards and stewardesses, who smilingly said, "We do apologize for this delay."

But a gloomy second-class passenger found an empty bottle of Riesling and stuffed a rolled note inside it that read: "We are run aground one hour, every minute terrific thumping. At least one lifeboat and passengers already gone. D. J. Behring, Mrs. Behring, Bremerhaven. I believe we are lost. I die in peace with my God and without anxiety. Love to friends, children, and mother-in-law." Herr Behring ran across the weather deck to hurl the corked Riesling bottle as far as he could into the sea. Three days later it washed up in a fishing village on the Colne River. By then *The Times* of London had published a list of the *Deutschland*'s survivors. D. J. Behring's name was on it; his wife's was not.

•

On the sultry morning of July 22nd, 1877, Hopkins endured an hour-long oral examination in moral and dogmatic theology. Just a year earlier a letter from the Jesuit Superior General in Italy had scolded the faculty of Saint Beuno's for their leniency in grading and for producing theologians who "could not adequately discriminate among various doctrinal positions."

Because of the tightened standards, the interrogation was trickier than the candidates for ordination expected, and Hopkins had watched Sydney Smith exit the quarters of Reverend Bernhard Tepe in the Priests' Gallery in a tottering state of shock, with no sense of how he'd done.

And then Hopkins heard Reverend Tepe impatiently call, "Gerardus Hopkins," and he entered.

Hopkins had never visited the professor's room and was stunned when he saw high walls of books culled from the libraries of Jesuit institutes that Otto von Bismarck had shut down; a huge harvest of words, wedged and stacked and ledged and spilling, filling even crannies and nooks, and squared like an ottoman in front of a plum-colored wingback chair. Sitting there was Bernhard Tepe, a portly, soft man with the pink-cheeked round face of an Italian putto and fluent, silky hair that was prematurely white. On a purple velvet sofa and fanning himself was Reverend Viktor Frins, a scowling, hawkish scholar with silvery eyes who was an exile from Germany, and Reverend William Hayden, an Englishman who was just two class years ahead of Hopkins and was overcompensating for his junior status with studied joylessness. Reverend Emilio Perini, an Italian professor of Hebrew and Sacred Scripture who was even shorter than Hopkins, held the door and offered the examinee a handshake that was fleet, moist, and weak, and then indicated a central Windsor chair on which Hopkins sat stiffly with his shoes flat on the oak floor and his hands on his cassocked thighs, just as he'd been instructed to do as a novice.

The examination was in Latin and commenced with Bernhard Tepe casually asking how the general themes of change, dependence, contingency, limited perfection, and utility were at the root of Thomas Aquinas's five ways to prove the existence of God. A freshman in philosophy could have answered him with ease. Emilio Perini then questioned Hopkins on Aristotle's *Nichomachean Ethics,* Aquinas's philosophical commentaries on them, and how his thinking there affected moral theology in the nineteenth century. Hearing him out, Viktor Frins wanted to know how the Church's doctrine on the Holy Trinity had evolved since Boethius's *De Trinitate,* and William Hayden detected something in his answer that incited him to have the theologian consider Peter Lombard's *Sentences.*

Rather than citing Aquinas's treatise on the *Sentences,* Hopkins gave in to his renegade partiality for the theology of the thirteenth-century Franciscan Johannes Duns Scotus and his Oxford commentary on Peter Lombard in *Opus Oxoniense.* Bernhard Tepe seemed peeved by that, but shifted to the Christology enunciated at the Council of Chalcedon, that the person of Jesus united his divinity and his humanity without blending them into a third reality. Hopkins provided a general exposition of the doctrine, which would have been enough for his examiners, but then he sought to overcome their ignorance of Duns Scotus by detailing the Oxford theologian's nuanced rejection of Aquinas's metaphysics in explaining the one personality of Christ in which his two natures are united. And in spite of his examiners' worries and mystification, the wild contrarian in him won out and Hopkins pressed on with his enthusiasm, interrupting their scrutinies in a manic exertion to make them as excited about Duns Scotus as he was when he first read him on *haecceitas*, or "thisness," in philosophy studies at Stonyhurst. He even switched from Latin to English to say, "Scotus saw too far, he knew too much; his subtlety overshot his own interests. A kind of feud arose between his genius and talent, and those who could not understand him voted that there was nothing important to understand, and so first misquoted him and then refuted him."

Ever afterward, Hopkins would defend his own poetry in much the same way.

Examiner William Hayden warned in English, "We seem to have gone far afield in our inquiries."

But the room was hot, and when Reverend Bernhard Tepe announced their hour was concluded, Reverend Viktor Frins immediately stood up and turned his back to the examinee as he tilted out the tall opened window for some zephyrs of air.

Exiting, Hopkins overheard William Hayden confide to Reverend Emilio Perini a compliment about Hopkins and "the pestering originality of his intellect," but the scowls and side glances among the other examiners were enough to convince him his examination was a wreck. Heading downstairs to the main chapel, he inched himself out facedown on the cool marble floor and scourged himself with "Stupid, stupid, stupid." And so he was not surprised when he learned he was given negative marks by two of the four examiners, which meant that Hopkins would not continue at Saint Beuno's for the fourth year of theology that was necessary for major offices in the Society of Jesus. He was, as Joseph Rickaby put it, "plucked."

•

Nine months earlier Reverend James Jones had been made Superior of the British Province, essentially swapping his job at Saint Beuno's with the ex-Provincial Peter Gallwey, who had been a concerned and much-loved Rector of Manresa House in Roehampton when Hopkins was a novice there.

Ever nervous about the examination results for his theologians, Rector Gallwey was pacing his worn office rug when Hopkins reported his score. "Oh, Gerard," he said. "I am so sorry."

Hopkins's face seemed bleached with the humiliation of it, but he constructed a smile of wonder. "It's the first time I've ever failed a subject. I feel distinctly misjudged."

"But you'll still be ordained a priest in September," Gallwey said. "You can't dwell on this to the exclusion of that."

"Pip pip, hooray," Hopkins said, and later scolded himself for it.

•

Three days later Hopkins was given a fortnight's holiday at his family's Oak Hill home in Hampstead and visited James Jones, now the British Provincial, in his headquarters in London, not far from Hyde Park. The higher office had forced on the hale and hearty Jones reticence and aloneness; he felt disconnected from his Jesuit brothers and overburdened by his chores, his financial constraints, and jobs that were multiplying with too few men to fill them.

Though he'd been friendly with Jones at Saint Beuno's, Hopkins was not unlike those other Jesuits when he visited the Provincial to hear his assignment. Stiff, awkward, and shy, he was there to talk about his future in the Society of Jesus and blunderingly started one hare after another and only met silence or a quenching utterance. But at last as Hopkins finished his breakfast and put his dish and silverware on a sideboard, Jones let go of his embarrassment to say, "Are you aware of the position of bursar?"

"The business officer at a college."

"We have need of one at Mount Saint Mary's," Jones said, folding his napkin, not looking up. "You'd be teaching occasional classes, too. And there would be priestly ministries, of course."

"In Yorkshire." Jones, he realized, was aware the job was one for which he was ill suited and would seem a penance for his weak examination. Hopkins shrugged. "If that's what God wants me to do."

"I have no idea," Jones said. "I just sort men out. We don't always get to do what we want in our least Society."

"And you? Are you doing what you want?"

Jones twitched a smile and quoted from Vergil's *Aeneid*: "'Perhaps at some later date we shall remember these things with fondness.'"

•

On the weekend, Hopkins was invited to Bedford Square for dinner in the magnificent Georgian home of his Oxford classmate Robert Seymour Bridges, who was then a house physician at Saint Bartholomew's Hospital in London. His father had died when Bridges was just a boy, and though he was the eighth of nine children, there was still enough of an inheritance that a job and a livelihood were never nettlesome questions for Dr. Bridges, and for much of his life he would be a gentleman of leisure. He was over six feet tall and wide-shouldered, a man's man who had played football and cricket and was the star oarsman for the Corpus Christi College rowing team; at Oxford he'd been considered so stunningly handsome that some classmates could not take their eyes off him. And if he was cold, secretive, aggressively intolerant, and given to petulant exhibitions of rudeness—or, put kindly, "delightfully grumpy"—he was also softhearted, considerate, and highly musical.

On that July evening, Bridges uncorked a bottle of Tre-bujena sherry and played songs on the piano and violin for his friend as the cook put out their dinner of tomato soup, fillets of plaice, and parsley-garnished potatoes. Bridges called himself an Anglican, but was increasingly agnostic, so they avoided the subject of religion during the meal and instead concentrated on their mutual love of John Keats, John Milton, and the seventeenth-century English composer Henry Purcell. After dinner Bridges stood next to his piano's silver candelabrum to read selections from his new collection of poetry, *The Growth of Love*, and then, like a schoolboy on tenterhooks, hunched forward in his Queen Anne chair to hear Hopkins's praise and recommendations.

Hopkins had only discovered that the very private Bridges wrote poetry in January 1874, when he was reading an issue of the literary journal *The Academy* and was stunned to find on page 53 a review of *Poems* by Robert Bridges, an author praised for "a fancy that can be strange when it chooses, and has always a power of delicate surprise, simplicity, courtliness, feeling, and music of no vulgar order." Weekly community encounters within the Society of Jesus—so-called fraternal corrections—had instilled in Hopkins the invaluable gift of candor, and he was so frank in his criticisms of that first book, but also so gracious and perceptive in his esteem, that Bridges had begun to depend on Hopkins's judgments as the only ones he trusted.

Without conceit, Hopkins told Bridges that night, "In general, I don't think you have reached finality yet in execution. Words might be chosen with more point and propriety. Images might be more brilliant." But he found a good deal of beauty in *The Growth of Love* and generously lauded Bridges for his "manly tenderness" and "flowing and never-failing music."

Still, Bridges was stung, and when his silence forced Hopkins to veer the conversation to his own poetry writing, Bridges handsomely grinned and said, "I insist I see something soon so I can have at it."

"I shall await your scolding," Hopkins said. And the next morning mailed his handwritten manuscript of "The Wreck of the Deutschland," adding in a note to Bridges, "Much against my inclination I shall have to leave Wales."

•

Hopkins's holiday just outside London lasted three weeks. Waking at five in the large Oak Hill house on his final day, with those he called "the parentage" still asleep, Hopkins strolled the backyard gardens in pajamas and his father's silk robe, his father's old calfskin slippers blackening with the lawn's fleece of dew. Wisteria, flowers, stalks, and stems— all long and lovely and lush; the world full of juice and joy. Sunshine glinted off pints of new cream on the stoop. The scullery maid was filling a kettle with water. Soon the upstairs maid would be making his bed. A muchness of food would steam on the sideboard as his father spooned into his three-minute egg. Robert Bridges would be seeing to the night's casualties at Saint Bartholomew's Hospital. Other Oxford classmates would be heading to their offices in the financial district or in publishing houses and possibly making plans for dinner parties or the theater that evening. *Christ tempted in the desert,* Hopkins thought. *This could all be yours.*

Wearing his father's bowler hat and dark gabardine suit, Hopkins visited the National Portrait Gallery that afternoon with his brother Everard—who was sixteen years his junior and would much later name his firstborn son Gerard. But instead of going directly home with the teen who idolized him, Hopkins took the Underground railway to the London borough of Leytonstone and entered Saint Patrick's Cemetery from Langthorne Road. The superintendent directed him past soot-streaked angels and crowds of graying crosses and some vaguely Greek and Italian mausoleums to an area dedicated to the burial plots for the Sisters of Jesus and Mary in Chigwell, the Sisters of Mercy of Walthamstow, and the Ursuline Sisters of Upton. And then Hopkins found plot A13, grave number 373. White curbstones in the dimensions of a funeral bier contained a field of black pebbles, and at the head was a gleaming white limestone memorial that was as high as his chin and shaped like a church front topped by a cross. The inscription read:

PRAY FOR THE SOULS OF

BARBARA HULTENSCHMIDT

HENRICA FASSBENDER

NORBERTA REINKOBER

AUREA BADZIURA

BRIGITTA DAMMHORST

FRANCISCAN SISTERS FROM GERMANY

WHO WERE DROWNED NEAR HARWICH IN THE WRECK

OF THE DEUTSCHLAND DEC 7TH 1875

FOUR OF WHOM WERE INTERRED HERE DEC 13TH

R - I - P

Hopkins felt a pang of regret for not having given their names in his poem, but he prayed that he had otherwise done them justice, and he requested their intercession so that he forever onward would be a good priest. And then a stanza of his ode interrupted him. Was it the twenty-fourth? His favorite.

> Away in the loveable west,
> On a pastoral forehead of Wales,
> I was under a roof here, I was at rest,
> And they the prey of the gales;
> She to the black-about air, to the breaker, the thickly
> Falling flakes, to the throng that catches and quails
> Was calling 'O Christ, Christ, come quickly':
> The cross to her she calls Christ to her, christens her wild-worst Best.

But it did not seem right to end his visit with his own words, so he got his rosary beads out of his father's suitcoat pocket and solemnly stood before the grave to pray the Sorrowful Mysteries of Christ's passion and death, but smiling and cringing at the melodrama of a nearby gardener's sour scythe regularly ringing as it sliced through hanks of grass.

•

In 1918, Robert Bridges introduced his collation of the *Poems of Gerard Manley Hopkins* with this footnote on "The Wreck of the Deutschland":

> The labour spent on this great metrical experiment must have served to establish the poet's prosody and perhaps his diction: therefore the poem stands logically as well as chronologically in the front of his book, like a great dragon folded in the gate to forbid all entrance, and confident in his strength from past success. This editor advises the reader to circumvent him and attack him later in the rear; for he was himself shamefully worsted in a brave frontal assault, the more easily perhaps because both subject and treatment were distasteful to him.

It was in such a mood that Robert Bridges wrote his Oxford classmate about the poem in 1877, for Hopkins replied in an August 21st letter from Saint Beuno's:

> Your parody reassures me about your understanding the metre. Only remark, as you say that there is no conceivable licence I shd. not be able to justify, that with all my licences, or rather laws, I am stricter than you and, I might say, than anybody I know. With the exception of the *Bremen* stanza, which was, I think, the first written after 10 years' interval of silence, and before I had fixed my principles, my rhymes are rigidly good—to the ear—and such rhymes as "love" and "prove" I scout utterly . . .

You ask may you call it "presumptious jugglery." No, but only for this reason, that presumptious is not English.

I cannot think of altering anything. Why shd. I? I do not write for the public. You are my public and I hope to convert you.

You say you wd. not for any money read my poem again. Nevertheless I beg you will. Besides money, you know, there is love. If it is obscure do not bother yourself with the meaning but pay attention to the best and most intelligible stanzas, as the two last of each part and the narrative of the wreck. If you had done this you wd. have liked it better and sent me some serviceable criticisms, but now your criticism is of no use, being only a protest memorialising me against my whole policy and proceedings.

I may add for your greater interest and edification that what refers to myself in the poem is all strictly true and did all occur; nothing is added for poetical padding.

Believe me your affectionate friend,

GERARD M. HOPKINS, S.J.

5

> She drove in the dark to leeward,
>   She struck—not a reef or a rock
>   But the combs of a smother of sand: night drew her
>   Dead to the Kentish Knock;
>   And she beat the bank down with her bows and the ride of her keel:
>   The breakers rolled on her beam with ruinous shock;
>   And canvas and compass, the whorl and the wheel
> Idle for ever to waft her or wind her with, these she endured.

•

At eight o'clock on the morning of December 6th, the five Sisters gathered in Sister Henrica's quarters for "The Little Office of the Blessed Virgin Mary," which they'd postponed. Tears trickled down Sister Brigitta's face throughout the recitation of the Psalms. Sister Barbara stood tall and stalwart, without hint of emotion. Sister Norberta glared out the porthole as if a terrible injustice against her was being urged and abetted. With no strong convictions of calamity, Sister Aurea cradled her Meissen doll and noticed the contrasting attitudes with wary curiosity.

Sister Henrica instructed the Sisters to sit as she opened

her Holy Bible to the Gospel According to Luke and read: "Now it came to pass on a certain day, that he went into a ship with his disciples: and he said unto them, Let us go over unto the other side of the lake. And they launched forth.

"But as they sailed he fell asleep: and there came down a storm of wind on the lake; and they were filled with water, and were in jeopardy.

"And they came to him, saying, Master, master, we perish. Then he arose, rebuked the wind and the raging of the water: and they ceased, and there was calm.

"And he said unto them, Where is your faith? And they being afraid wondered, saying to one another, What manner of man is this! for he commandeth even the winds and water, and they obey him."

She shut the book and sat in silent meditation with them for five minutes, until Sister Barbara, first, and then the others, prayerfully filed out.

•

Weary stewards were manning the hand pumps in steerage and the cargo hold until Carl Dietrich Meyer stripped down to his long underwear and sloshed down the corridor to spell one older man, vigorously pumping for a full five minutes until he lost his breath and had to tilt over, gasping, with his hands on his knees. Smiling at the steerage passengers who were silently watching, he said, "We need some spirited competition here! Five marks to the man who thinks he can out-pump me!"

Soon the rivalry was so great that men and boys were cheering their own and crowding up for their chance at the hand pumps, which kept the ship fairly free of water until nightfall.

The sea took pity. The swells slackened with the ebbing tide and the snow ceased, though the cold seemed worse and the wind, though softer, was incessant.

In the pilothouse, Captain Brickenstein was consulting his charts. The Kentish Knock was just a half-mile wide at their latitude, and he noted that smoother water was just two ship's lengths off. Cargo was jettisoned from the fore hatch in an effort to lift the prow of the *Deutschland* from the sandbank. Eventually the jetsam thrilled finders on the shore, with three hundred and sixty cases of gloves winding up near Margate on the Kent coast, and a case of silk washing ashore near Herne Bay. Crates of Meissen porcelain dolls gradually sank underwater and skidded down the slope of the Knock. With the ship's lightening, Brickenstein had the canvas foresail and topsail hoisted and watched in suspense as they fattened with wind. The *Deutschland* groaned loudly as the sails dragged it grindingly over the sandbank in a laggard progress of no more than thirty yards per hour.

Waiting for the rescue that they estimated could only be soon, some restless passengers sashayed in the rinsed morning air under sunshine and azure skies. Seamen shoveled and broomed away snow as if they had nothing better to do.

Twenty-one-year-old Adolf Hermann watched them work with the younger Anna Petzold, listening to the girl teach with stunning authority about most things American, particularly New York City, where her father was a surgeon. But she was secretly embarrassed that she could say nothing about Cincinnati, where Adolf was headed, so she distracted him from the great chasm of her ignorance by changing the subject to the territory of Alaska, where it was colder than this six months of the year, and the sun shone for hardly one hour per day, and houses were made with blocks of ice, and it was so cold, Adolf, that if Eskimos kissed, their mouths would stick together, so instead the Eskimos rubbed noses.

The shine in Anna's blue eyes when she mentioned kissing caused Adolf to hang his head in shyness.

She caught that and changed the subject again. "Cincinnati is nice," Anna Petzold confidently stated. "Many Germans are there."

A Swede named Olaf Lundgren stepped around the couple as he walked a hardy constitutional around the weather deck with the New Yorker Heymann Nathan and told him that in May, just seven months earlier, he'd been onboard the *Schiller*, a transatlantic liner that had wrecked on the Scilly Islands southwest of Land's End, England. Three hundred twelve people lost their lives.

"And you're here to tell the tale," Nathan said in English. "You're our good-luck charm."

"Perhaps yes," Lundgren dully said. "I hope so."

Nathan later recalled that they discussed the fishing catch off the Essex coast, which they thought was mostly blackwater herring and oysters. But in winter, Lundgren told him, the Harwich fishermen, called Scropers, sailed out to ships in distress to extricate the passengers and, uppermost in their minds, to salvage merchandise for premiums from the insurance companies. "Some strange fishing that is," said Olaf Lundgren, who would not survive.

Sister Henrica and Sister Brigitta strolled past the men, who tipped their hats, and they stood at the railing to look out on the slant ruck and crease of waves racing the wind and scrolling and overlapping each other, or twitching and tumbling like the canvas of a loose sail.

"The air smells so clean," Sister Brigitta said.

Sister Henrica inhaled it. "Like skiing in Innsbruck," she said.

"Austria! Have you been there?"

"Even Vienna."

Sister Brigitta pouted. "I haven't been anywhere."

"You'll be in England soon."

Sister Brigitta said nothing for a while. They walked toward the bow watching the hurl and gliding of a lone sea-gull whose wings wimpled as it rode the currents of air.

"I'm still afraid," Sister Brigitta admitted.

"Well, given the circumstances," Sister Henrica said, "that sounds quite sensible."

Sister Brigitta smiled at the psychology.

Sister Henrica smiled as well. "It is the happy duty of a Superior to always be a source of calm and reassurance."

The Sisters turned around near the foredeck, where August Lauenstein and Charles Dore Harvey were taking turns with a spyglass to observe seven sailors at their ordinary chores on the sailless Kentish Knock lightship that was anchored in warning three sea miles away. And then Lauenstein spyglassed the panorama and noticed a cargo ship steaming toward them from the southeast. But the ship strangely veered away when only a half-mile off. Lauenstein ran to his quarters and out again with a Colt revolver in order to waken the cargo ship's captain to their plight. He fired three pistol shots into the skies and was tempted to whang a bullet off the iron hull, but the ship was itself so flooded and overweight with water that its gunwales were only a foot above the sea and its master was himself doing whatever he could not to sink as the ship continued onward to the horizon with no sign of having seen or heard them.

The English Channel pilot reminded the irritated Lauenstein that these shipping lanes were quite possibly the busi-
est in the world, and within the hour Charles Dore Harvey
spyglassed in the east-northeast the speck of a brigantine
headed their way at a speed of three or four knots. Captained
by Thomas Key, the *Ino* was transporting a cargo of the
pine and fir planks that were called deal and was avoiding
the Kentish Knock as it steered toward the Strait of Dover
and England's southern port of Weymouth. But the *Ino* seemed
to be steaming directly toward them, and Lauenstein hurried
to the helm to alert the captain and crew of their deliver-
ance.

Word of a rescue vessel passed through the ship, and soon
fully dressed second-class passengers were lounging in the
grand saloon with their luggage. Coffee and sandwiches were
served. Jacobine Schwartz idly chatted with Edward Stamm
as her five-year-old, Adam, scurried around the furniture with
Stamm's six-year-old, Elise, the children still in their life vests
as they played tag. William B. Fundling was hunched on his
steamer trunk, scouring an accounting ledger for an error
in arithmetic, and his wife and daughter talked to Maria
Forster about the newly invented scents being advertised just
in time for Christmas at their Manhattan perfumery business.
Sister Barbara cooed as she rocked Anna Gmolch's daughter
Paulina, and Sister Aurea danced her doll for Babette Binder's
dazzled baby. Sister Norberta began reading Jules Verne's international best-seller *Around the World in Eighty Days*. And
she just didn't give a fig for what that snooty Sister Mary
Henrica would have to say about it.

•

Quartermaster August Bock, who was presumed lost at sea, was still clinging to life in his sloop. Seeing that the northeast wind was carrying them westward toward the English coast, he had fastened the clews of a sail to the hinged mast of the large wooden lifeboat, and he and Seaman Forsenstein hoisted the mast, chocking it upright with cleats. The sloop's sail grew pregnant with the wind, and Bock kept it bellied with a primitive tiller as they waited for rescue in the turbulence of the sea. Ships passed them without notice though Bock and Forsenstein shouted until their voices grew hoarse. The huddled, moaning passenger in the sloop's prow lost consciousness at noon on Monday, and soon, with no defense against the claims of exposure, he died.

Seaman Forsenstein was just eighteen and, as Bock later put it, "hadn't got inured to the hardships of the sea. I coaxed him and bullied him to move, so as to keep the blood going in his veins, but all to no purpose." Hurting with cold and weak with exhaustion, the seaman lost heart and crouched in a seizure of shivers as freezing water sloshed around his shoes, and when Bock massaged the boy's hugging shoulders and arms to warm him, Forsenstein's wet eyes looked up at him in pining silence and with a "helpless expression that gave me a chill all through, for I knew it meant nothing else but that death was coming."

With nightfall Bock stayed at the tiller, hunger and thirst his only company as he sought hints of land. His hands and feet became nearly useless with frostbite, for "the cold was something awful," and he did not realize Forsenstein had died until a big wave caused the sloop to lurch leeward and he saw the skull beneath the seaman's skin and his staring, unseeing eyes. Bock dutifully tied the tiller in place and tugged the seaman's limp body forward until it was conjugal with the stiffer corpse in the prow, and then he glumly returned to the stern, singing sailor's shanties throughout the wee hours in order to stay awake and alive.

At six o'clock on the morning of December 7th, a British sentry at the Royal Navy barracks in Sheerness noticed the sloop wobbling against the night-black beach. Stunned that a party of soldiers might have invaded their environment, the sentry and two other artillerymen rushed down to the seemingly empty sloop and discovered a hallucinatory and grateful quartermaster, who found the necessary vocabulary in English to explain himself and his two dead companions, their bodies now blackened by salt water and cold.

Hearing Bock's report of the shipwreck, a Navy telegraph operator alerted the coast guard station at Harwich about the *Deutschland*'s dire situation, but there was nothing the coast guard could do until there was a lull in the weather.

Carried to the naval infirmary, and then confined to a hospital bed, the grinning and hobbling August Bock became a celebrity in Sheerness, receiving so many gifts and jubilant visits from civic leaders and hero worshippers that he remained in England even beyond the period of his recuperation just to enjoy his new friends.

•

On three successive days in late September 1877, Hopkins and fifteen classmates were ordained by Bishop Brown of Shrewsbury to the Holy Orders of subdeacon, deacon, and priest. Hopkins was thirty-three years old, nine years a Jesuit, and honored and jubilant, though in their hostility to his faith no family members or friends attended Sunday's glorious ordination ceremony or the grand celebration in the refectory afterward. The new priests jokingly "father"ed each other excessively as six of the scholastics served tomato soup, sweet peas, French beans, roast mutton, ham, fowls, and a variety of wines to over fifty guests, who then strolled the lawns and went into the scholastics' recreation room to hear the school's string quartet play Vivaldi's *Four Seasons*. Looking on as the Splaine family crowded around their sons, as Rickaby's father the butler was proud as a lord, Hopkins finally permitted himself to fume over his family's shunning him, thinking, *This is my wedding and they aren't here.*

The next morning he celebrated his first Mass in the Saint Agnes oratory with only Joseph Rickaby's younger brother John, as acolyte, in attendance. But he was so thrilled at the Consecration that the Host shook in his hands and he could only stare with gratitude and awe as he recited the Latin words of Christ's institutional narrative, *"Hoc est enim corpus meum."* This is my body. And later, when he genuflected and shut the gold ciborium inside the tabernacle, he recalled "The Habit of Perfection," written at Oxford when he was still considering conversion: "But you shall walk the golden street / And you unhouse and house the Lord." The great privilege and wonder of it would never leave him.

Ten Saint Beuno's theologians would be staying on for a fourth year that would concentrate on nineteen centuries of Christian doctrine. Hopkins was one of six newly ordained priests who were technically called "Spiritual Coadjutors" rather than "Professed Fathers," and who he conjectured would be henceforward the genial, hardy, overworked donkeys in the enterprising British Province's ever more numerous and understaffed schools and ministries.

Mount Saint Mary's College was located near the Sheffield coal mines in Yorkshire, where in an uninteresting landscape and smoke-ridden air he was treasurer and subminister to the Prefect of Studies, taught Latin to eleven-to-thirteen-year-old boys and religion to two classrooms of upper-sixth-form students, in addition to hearing confessions, saying Mass, and giving retreats at the parish church. Within months he was writing Robert Bridges to request a return to him of the manuscript he called by the ship's name, *Deutschland*, "or she will in course of time be lost." *As he would be*, he thought.

Worried that he still cared too much about what ought to have been, for a priest, a hobby, he cultivated an air of nonchalance about his poems, mailing them off as if they were no more than scissored whimsies and yarns from village newspapers. But Reverend Francis Bacon in Glasgow, his classmate in the Novitiate, and Dr. Robert Bridges in London, whose many pastimes included calligraphy, were such good friends to his work that they provided the insurance of copying the poems out into their own albums.

There was no such protection for his teaching. In an age when boys were considered the direst enemies of learning, headmasters would continually grouse that Hopkins was too gentle with his pupils and gave them all the freedom of bookish undergraduates at Oxford, a latitude the boys abused with uproar and whistling, once shunting their desks forward as he chalked the blackboard, so that when he turned back to them he found himself corralled.

"Well," he said in his high tenor voice, "I must say I'm gratified by your keen interest in the Latin ablative case."

And there were other "originalities," as his Superior called them. Encountering a weeping boy in the yard, Hopkins sought to perk him up by flinging off his chalky, pleated schoolmaster's gown and, shoeless, in his suit, insanely shinnying up a football goalpost. Another time, having no fear of heights, Hopkins walked the third-story window ledge of a hall, casual as a cat, in order to rescue a boy's pet monkey. In one classroom he found a penciled caricature of himself in all his haggard hideousness, and increasingly as he strolled into the dining hall, he would hear some boy whisper, "There he is."

The ugliness of the Yorkshire landscape and the cold and foulness of the climate caused such sourness in him that he wrote Bridges: "Life here is as dank as ditch-water and has some of the other qualities of ditch-water: at least I know that I am reduced to great weakness by diarrhea, which lasts too, as if I were poisoned."

So he was happy to be relocated to Stonyhurst College in May in order to coach lay pupils for their philosophy examinations at the University of London. But his "mess of employments" still meant he wrote no poetry in six months as a priest until he read of three-hundred-sixty-six seamen and boys lost on the frigate H.M.S. *Eurydice* in a training cruise that ended in a March squall and snowstorm off the Isle of Wight. With greater speed, but fewer examples of genius, he imagined another shipwreck and wrote a one-hundred-twenty-line narrative he entitled "The Loss of the Eurydice."

Stung that *The Month* rejected that, too, Hopkins sought out a sympathetic correspondence with a Church of England clergyman who'd been an assistant master at Highgate School and whose book of poems, *Christ's Company*, Hopkins had read and admired at Oxford. Worrying that it could have been construed an impertinence to contact Canon Richard Watson Dixon, he still thought he should, for:

I seemed to owe you something or a great deal, and then I knew what I should feel myself in your position—if I had written and published works the extreme beauty of which the author himself the most keenly feels and they had fallen out of sight at once and been (you will not mind my saying it, as it is, I suppose, plainly true) almost wholly unknown; then, I say, I should feel a certain comfort to be told they had been deeply appreciated by some one person, a stranger, at all events and had not been published quite in vain. Many beautiful works have been almost unknown and then have gained fame at last . . . but many more must have been lost sight of altogether. I do not know of course whether your books are going to have a revival, it seems not likely, but not for want of deserving. It is not that I think a man is really the less happy because he has missed the renown which was his due, but still when this happens it is an evil in itself and a thing which ought not to be and that I deplore, for the good work's sake rather than the author's . . .

Richard Watson Dixon gratefully wrote back, recalling at Highgate "a pale young boy, very light and active, with a very meditative & intellectual face, whose name, if I am not vastly mistaken, was yours. If I am not deceived by memory, that boy got a prize for English poetry."

In his June 1878 reply, Hopkins spoke of fame as "a great danger in itself, as dangerous as wealth every bit."

And even if it does not lead men to break the divine law, yet it gives them "itching ears" and makes them live on public breath.

What I do regret is the loss of recognition belonging to the work itself. For as to every moral act, being right or wrong, there belongs, of the nature of things, reward or punishment, so to every form perceived by the mind belongs, of the nature of things, admiration or the reverse. And the world is full of things and events, phenomena of all sorts, that go without notice, go unwitnessed . . .

It is sad to think what disappointment must many times over have filled your heart for the darling children of your mind. Nevertheless fame whether won or lost is a thing which lies in the award of a random, reckless, incompetent, and unjust judge, the public, the multitude. The only just judge, the only just literary critic, is Christ, who prizes, is proud of, and admires, more than any man, more than the receiver himself can, the gifts of his own making.

•

In July Hopkins was transferred to the Jesuit headquarters and hidden parish church near Grosvenor Square, London, and wrote his friend Bridges that he presumed his residence there would be permanent, "but permanence with us is gingerbread permanence; cobweb, soapsud, and frost-feather permanence."

Writing a mutual friend from his home on Bedford Square, Bridges noted that "Gerard Hopkins is in town preaching & confessing at Farm Street. I went to hear him: he is good. He calls here: and we have sweet laughter, and pleasant chats. He is not at all the worse for being a Jesuit, as far as one can judge without knowing what he would have been otherwise." And he added, "His poetry is magnificent but 'caviare to the general'"—a phrase Bridges borrowed from Shakespeare that meant the public would not like it.

•

Just five months after establishing himself in London, Hopkins was again uprooted and sent to Saint Aloysius Church in Oxford. Writing Bridges, he asked that his handwritten copies of "The Wreck of the Deutschland" and "The Loss of the Eurydice" be mailed to Reverend Cyprian Splaine, for he had "expressed a curiosity to see my two almost famous Rejected Addresses."

An old classmate, Francis de Paravicini, was still at Oxford as a Fellow, and he and his wife joined Hopkins in sculling the green, slow Cherwell River, their boats sliding with a satiny, Elysian motion beneath the hanging tresses of willows. Hopkins dined with Renaissance scholar Walter Pater in his house, but whenever his former tutor, an atheist, chanced to notice Hopkins's Roman collar, his eyes seemed to stumble as if he'd been hexed. The educated elites and the upper classes had been Hopkins's primary company in his undergraduate years at Oxford; now he was "Reverend Father" to shopkeepers and grunt laborers who esteemed their priests and conscientiously took part in their ceremonies, but who seemed "as if a joke from us would put them to deep and lasting pain."

An 1879 wet-plate photograph was taken of Hopkins standing in front of Saint Aloysius Church with his John Bullish pastor and thirteen men in the Oxford Catholic Club: Hopkins tilting backward against the bricks, his hairline receding, his face wan and shaven and haughty. He seemed frail, little, joyless, exhausted—a lofty ecclesiastic so seemingly unconnected to the others that his image could have been a photographer's trick, an insertion.

•

Within ten months of his arrival—in which time he wrote ten poems, including "Duns Scotus's Oxford" and "Binsey Poplars"—he was uninserted from Oxford and sent for six weeks to the stinking, "darksome" foundry town of Bedford Leigh, and then to Saint Francis Xavier Parish in the slums of the industrial city of Liverpool, "a most unhappy and miserable spot." Bill Dubberley, Hopkins's Saint Beuno's classmate, joined him at Saint Francis Xavier and was the greater success with parishioners, who considered Hopkins a highbrowed intellectual whose sermons were either sentimental or perplexing, and who once sinned to the pastor's ears by calling Jesus a "Sweetheart."

And still he felt ill and overworked. Chilblains affected him. He treated a tooth abscess with leeches. Writing to Bridges about not writing, Hopkins sighed that "time and spirits were wanting; one is so fagged, so harried and gallied up and down. And the drunkards go on drinking, the filthy, as the scripture says, are filthy still: human nature is so inveterate. Would that I had seen the last of it."

But misanthropy was not characteristic of him, and two of his tenderest poems were written in Liverpool: "Felix Randal," about a "hardy-handsome" farrier in Lancashire to whom Hopkins ministered as he was dying, and "Spring and Fall: To a Young Girl," of a child's first faint intimations of mortality in September's fall of leaves.

In October 1881 he returned to Roehampton in southwest London for the ordinary near-year of tertianship at Manresa House, a gardened estate overlooking Richmond Park where the Prince Regent once lived. In that variation on the Novitiate retreat experience, the *Spiritual Exercises* were repeated in the context of the Jesuit's past ministries, and the bulk of each day was given over to prayer and study. Hopkins wrote Canon Dixon that "my mind is here more at peace than it has ever been and I would gladly live all my life, if it were so to be, in as great or a greater seclusion from the world and be busied only with God."

On August 15th, 1882, the Feast of the Assumption, Hopkins professed his final vows of poverty, chastity, and obedience, completing his formal training as a Jesuit in the place where he'd commenced it fourteen years earlier. And just as he had gone from the Novitiate to Stonyhurst for philosophy studies, he was now sent to Stonyhurst College to again coach lay undergraduates for their baccalaureate examinations. But by July of the next year, he was writing Bridges:

> It seems likely that I shall be removed; where I have no notion. But I have long been Fortune's football and am blowing up the bladder of resolution big and buxom for another kick of her foot. I shall be sorry to leave Stonyhurst; but go or stay, there is no likelihood of my ever doing anything to last. And I do not know how it is, I have no disease, but I am always tired, always jaded, though work is not heavy, and the impulse to do anything fails me or has in it no continuance.

•

The situation of the *Deutschland* was becoming increasingly desperate by nightfall on Monday, December 6th. Crew and passengers had watched the *Ino* in its snail-paced approach for three full hours and were on the weather deck with their trunks and bundles, readied for its slide alongside them, when, with rescue seemingly just a mile away, Captain Brickenstein told the helmsman, "You'd have to be monumentally stupid to jeopardize your ship in these shallows." And within minutes he watched the *Ino* steer east of the treacherous waters of the Kentish Knock and continue on toward the Strait of Dover, like a queen avoiding embarrassment.

Charles Dore Harvey took the spyglass from August Lauenstein and squinted through it until he could read the *Ino*'s name. And then in English he reminded Edward Stamm, who was beside him, that in classical mythology Ino was the sea goddess who rescued Odysseus from drowning.

Edward Stamm crossly replied that such delicious ironies might have been lost on his frightened six-year-old daughter.

With the rising tide, the hull was shipping water in such great volume that Captain Brickenstein was worried that once the ship slid off the Kentish Knock in its laggard progress toward calmer waters, the grossly overweight stern would sag undersea and sink them. And so, hating the hazard of it, Brickenstein anchored the ship while it was still aground, tilted forecastle downward, and in surf. Rockets that were called maroons were shot up into the night.

David Day, the mate of the Sunk lightship, watched the red flare and floral burst of the *Deutschland*'s rocket and ordered a seaman to reply with one of their own, though it was his thought, as he said at the inquest later, that "no boat could live in that water. The Sunk was hurled about as much as I had ever known her to be."

The Kentish Knock lightship also answered with a rocket, and all were recorded by the coast guard station at Harwich. But there was nothing more they could do.

Siegfried Benning, the ship's purser, stopped in the pilothouse to say the passengers were asking just what the rocket signals meant.

"They mean misery loves company," Eduard Brickenstein said.

The continuous stunning shocks of crashing breakers were widening the seams in the iron skin of the ship, so that seawater filled the engine room and stokehold, dousing the coals in the furnace. The steam water pumps in turn were stopped and steerage was soon flooded. The small population still holding out down there was forced to hurry to the upper decks, cluttering the first- and second-class corridors with themselves and their patched, matchwood, worldly goods. Crew hauled up hundreds of soggy canvas bags of mail and stacked them in the gangways. And as the *Deutschland* took on more water, it became so gravid that it could not lift on the tide but formed its own reef for the seas to surge over. The stern was only five feet higher than the onrush, everything headmost was submerged. She was "tail up with an ear cocked," Mate Lauenstein said.

Class distinctions ended by eleven p.m., and the upper-class library, music room, and main saloon became as crowded and rowdy as chilly railway stations. With a new tide surging in at a velocity of two and a half knots, the sea seeped upward, the plush, intricate Axminster carpets squishing beneath the shoes of the stewards as they delivered sandwiches and sweet cakes and tulip glasses of Riesling.

The *Deutschland* was jolted again with the ram of a wave as the five Sisters waited for rescue in the saloon, sitting on their five black portmanteaus in their cloaks and life vests and reciting the night prayers of "The Little Office of the Blessed Virgin Mary." And this time Sister Henrica read from the Gospel According to Matthew: "And straightway Jesus constrained his disciples to get into a ship, and to go before him unto the other side, while he sent the multitudes away. And when he had sent the multitudes away, he went up into a mountain apart to pray: and when the evening was come, he was there alone. But the ship was now in the midst of the sea, tossed with waves: for the wind was contrary. And in the fourth watch of the night Jesus went unto them, walking on the sea. And when the disciples saw him walking on the sea, they were troubled, saying, It is a spirit; and they cried out in fear. But straightway, Jesus spake unto them, saying, Be of good cheer; it is I; be not afraid. And Peter answered him and said, Lord, if it be thou, bid me come unto thee on the water. And he said, Come. And when Peter was come down out of the ship, he walked on the water, to go to Jesus. But when he saw the wind boisterous, he was afraid; and beginning to sink, he cried, saying, Lord, save me. And immediately Jesus stretched forth his hand, and caught him, and saith unto him, O thou of little faith, wherefore didst thou doubt? And when they were come into the ship, the wind ceased. Then they that were in the ship came and worshipped him, saying, Of a truth thou art the Son of God."

She shut her Bible, and the five were sitting in silence, meditating on the Scripture, when a runnel of seawater slithered into the saloon and widened so that surprised passengers hopped aside of its lake or jerked their shoes up from the floor.

Close to midnight, Second Officer Carl Thalenhorst tilted inside the saloon and yelled, "All crew and passengers upstairs to the weather deck!"

The stewardess Catharina Schlossbauer immediately got a white napkin and waved it overhead like a tour guide as she commanded the hundred and more to leave their belongings and form up in pairs so she could conduct them in accordance with the captain's wishes.

"Shall we go?" Sister Barbara asked.

Sister Henrica was puzzled. "We have no choice."

"We could be disobedient," Sister Norberta said.

"But then we would not be good nuns."

"Won't it be cold?" Sister Aurea asked.

"No, it'll be hot," Sister Norberta acidly said. "Hot as Hades. You'll want a parasol, and a fan."

"Sister. Shush," Sister Brigitta said.

"Don't you 'shush' me."

"Sisters!" Sister Henrica said.

Sister Norberta stood beside Sister Barbara as she put on her mittens, snidely repeating, "Won't it be cold . . ."

Sister Henrica was stationed in front of the four nuns and paired with the ship's doctor, Franz Bluen, who was gloved and hatted and irritatedly winding a long woolen scarf around his neck. "Thalenhorst should have announced the rescue boat was here," he told her. "This peremptory ordering of the whole lot of us upstairs just keeps us in suspense."

"So it *is* here?"

Another jolt of a wave tipped him off-balance and he righted himself. "Certainly," Bluen said.

She recalled queuing up like this at the School of the Holy Cross in Aachen. She'd just received Holy Communion and she was praying as the Holy Cross Sisters put the girls in orderly rows for their entrance into school. And high up there on the landing of a steep flight of stairs was Wilhelm Fassbender, the eighth-grade teacher, Catharina's adoring father, who smiled down at his daughter and widened his arms in welcome.

Elderly Dr. Bluen gripped her elbow in a gentlemanly manner to help her up the gangway, though it was he who pawed the handrail in his struggle up the steps. Shocking cold hit them once they exited the hatchway. And there was no other vessel. Dr. Bluen was outraged. Some passengers were scurrying to the gaslit pilothouse and crowding into its heated parlor; some were in a hopeless wander or holding on to the fence around the giant funnel.

A great wave boomed against the ship, and cannoning white seawater that seemed high and heavy as a house hit Sister Henrica full on, joining her to its onwardness. She screamed and could hear other men and women screaming as she and they were carried on the raft of its swift, stinging journey across the width of the ship. She flailed in a last chance for the ship's railing, but she was plunged over the side of the *Deutschland* and into the coldest cold of water she'd ever felt. She lost all air; she lost a shoe; she could not tell up from down. She was suffering and terrified and helpless, and she could not claw up to the surface. Her black veil smothered her face, her black cloak furled around her like the strips of burial cloths binding Lazarus in his tomb, and she could not help it, she gasped, and seawater filled her. She coughed and convulsed and took in more. Weakening and in pain, she slashed out with her hands and kicked her feet in the finality of a wild rage. But she was burdened and yoked by her habit, and demanded by the sea. She remembered as she sank: Jesus wept.

Sister Mary Henrica Fassbender, F.C.J.M. (1847–1875)

•

Eduard Brickenstein noted that it was now just after midnight on Tuesday, December 7th, which meant he had not slept in thirty hours. And he felt he was hallucinating as he stood at the helm and watched the swells grow into giants, then avalanche across his ship in seething, roiling spumes of white foam. The stewardess whom the captain knew only by surname—Schlossbauer, he thought—was upended by a swell and speedily swept like a toy boat across the ship's beam, until she was wedged between railings and saved. Each wave that crashed in seemed to claim a life, and the shrieking pandemonium in front of him and the cries and weeping of those jammed inside the pilothouse were misery to the captain, who could do nothing more than witness it all. The December gale increased, and August Lauenstein took the megaphone outside and shouted for the crew and passengers to get into the riggings. Siegfried Benning, the ship's purser with nine years' service on the *Deutschland*, provided good example by immediately stepping up onto a railing and then onto a taut horizontal rope. Though he was now grossly overweight, Benning was trained as a boy in sail, and with old practice he nimbly ascended high up into a roost in the mainmast's shrouds and called down for others to join him.

But some passengers seemed to be retreating to the illusory safety of the saloon. Halting in the hatchway were the Salzkotten nuns, who'd watched in horror as Sister Henrica went tossing across the deck in a stampede of white water until she'd simply disappeared. Sister Aurea couldn't stop screeching. Sister Brigitta held the child of her and softly petted her veiled head, saying, "Shush now. Shh. Shh." Sister Norberta wailed in prayer, kissing her rosary's crucifix and holding it tight to her heart.

Sister Barbara, at thirty-two the oldest, considered her desolate sisters and decided she was their Superior now. She seriously asked, "Sister Norberta, will you be able to climb the riggings?"

The stricken woman sobbed as she considered the rope webbing overhead. "I'm too fat. I can't. I'll fall."

"We'll go down, then," Sister Barbara told the three, and they obediently descended the gangway, sloshing in icy, calf-high seawater as they returned to the saloon.

Others were there, children and wives and husbands squatting on Biedermeier tables, or perched higher on café chairs they'd put on the tables, their shoes dangling over the rising water like the shoes of fishermen on a bridge. Sister Barbara chose a wide round table, and the Sisters got up on it and seated themselves back to back. "Like a starfish," Sister Brigitta said.

Sister Aurea wiped her eyes and asked, "Is she dead?"

"She's a good swimmer, I think," Sister Brigitta told her.

"I'm so afraid for her," Sister Aurea said.

Sister Norberta snapped, "Stop it! You say such stupid things! Why are you always talking?"

She hugged herself tight. "I'm just sad. And so cold."

"We're all sad. We're all cold," Sister Norberta said.

Sister Aurea stonily faced her. "I loved Sister Henrica. She was nice."

> Hope had grown gray hairs,
>   Hope had mourning on,
> Trenched with tears, carved with cares,
>   Hope was twelve hours gone;
> And frightful a nightfall folded rueful a day
> Nor rescue, only rocket and lightship, shone,
>   And lives at last were washing away:
> To the shrouds they took,—they shook in the hurling and horrible
>   airs.

•

Earlier, Hopkins sought to explain his continuing movements to his mother by writing:

> Much change is inevitable, for every year so many people must begin and so many more must have ended their studies and it is plain that these can seldom step into the shoes left by those, so there is an almost universal shift. Then besides there are offices of fixed term, like Lord-mayoralties or Septennates. Add deaths, sicknesses, leavings, foreign missions, and what not and you will see that ours can never be an abiding city nor any one of us know what a day may bring forth; and it is our pride to be ready for instant despatch.

But Hopkins felt all the antonyms of pride on being posted to Ireland. His final move.

Reverend Edwin Purbrick was then the British Provincial, and though each week he dutifully dined or strolled with many of his Jesuit brothers, the encounters were notoriously and excruciatingly one-sided. One scholastic's anxiety was so great that he rehearsed an hour's conversation which he tore through at a breakfast table as Purbrick merely munched dry toast or delicately sipped his lukewarm tea, and when at last the scholastic was spent, Purbrick settled his teacup in its saucer and said, "Your last remark was singularly commonplace." And another priest whose interests were in chemistry, mathematics, and physics—in which Purbrick had little preparation or interest—composed a monologue on those subjects only to hear the British Provincial sigh and say, "How I hate *learning*."

And now Reverend William Delany, the Jesuit president of University College in Dublin, had contacted the British Provincial to recruit Hopkins as a junior professor of classics. Were the English Jesuit, with his Oxford first in "Greats," accepted for the job, the post carried with it a fellowship of four hundred pounds sterling from the Royal University of Ireland, an income that would cut in half the struggling college's annual losses. Edwin Purbrick cautioned Delany in his initial letter about the recruitment that even though Hopkins was "very clever and a good scholar," he was also so eccentric that the Provincial was presently trying him with the baccalaureate candidates at Stonyhurst "with fear and trembling."

Even with Hopkins sitting across from him in his Province office on Farm Street, Purbrick was scornful, treating him like a truant boy and scowling at his occasional comments as if they were interruptions. "Shall I share with you a copy of my letter of recommendation?" he asked. And before Hopkins could vote, the older man was reading: " 'I have no objection to your inviting Father Gerald Hopkins—' "

Hopkins corrected, "Gerard."

Purbrick squinted at the page and considered his error. "*Gerard*, is it? Well, no matter. 'Hopkins to stand as a candidate for a fellowship.' Ta da, ta *da*, I continue: 'I have the highest opinion of his scholarship and abilities. I fancy also that university work would be more in his line than anything else.' "

"Thank you," the candidate for a fellowship said.

The Provincial tilted his head down to stare at Hopkins over the rims of his spectacles. "Shall I go on?"

"There's more?"

"Oh yes. Here. 'Sometimes what we in Community deem

oddities are the very qualities which outside are appreciated as original and valuable.'"

"Oddities."

"Would you have me enumerate them?"

"I shall deny you that pleasure, Reverend Father."

But his Superior would not be denied. "Hiding in the Rector's closet to scare him with a 'Boo.' Other so-called practical jokes, such as disrupting a private committee meeting by fluting snuff through the keyhole. Crawling on your hands and knees during an outdoor commencement in pursuit of four-leaf clovers. Having your class drag you by the heels across the floor, howling, to demonstrate a description in the *Iliad*. Witty at times, yes. Entertaining for the students. But undignified and freakish, don't you agree?"

Hopkins said nothing.

"I do so hope you get the Dublin post and have the chance for a new start."

Hopkins smiled. "With each instant I find the job becoming more appealing."

•

But he was a Conservative in politics, like his father, and he disdained the Irish campaign for independence from the British Empire he still held dear. And Irish immigrants were commonly the objects of jokes and dismay, scorned in high society as drunken, stupid, and unwashed. Hopkins visited Oak Hill at Christmas and suffered his father's sneers at the possibility of the new assignment, his mother's fretfulness over his health and safety in a smoky city with a high mortality rate due to infectious diseases such as consumption and typhoid.

And there had been quarrels over him. Because of his Englishness, Hopkins's appointment was also opposed by the Cardinal Archbishop of Dublin, who felt there were too many non-Irish at University College. But Reverend Delany insisted on the hire, and in a volcanic January meeting of the Royal University senate, Hopkins was elected, with the Cardinal Archbishop and his nationalist successor resigning from the senate in protest.

In February 1884, Hopkins went alone with his trunk of clothing and books to Euston Station and boarded the northwestern railway to Holyhead, Wales. Sitting in an overheated second-class coach with his breviary, he glumly watched England slide past his window: snow in the fields and sodden, pillowy gray quilts of cloud hanging so close they seemed just out of reach of his hand, hurdles of black poplar trees ducking and eddying with the wind, the shanties of Irish immigrant workers crowding the rails near every village, and then the grim brown slums outside Liverpool, the shallow and frail seaside town of Rhyl, the gray Irish Sea to his right with a lone sailboat scudding on it, and then the end of Wales at Holyhead, where children cheated the hungry seagulls by chucking snowballs to them rather than bread.

Walking the pier at Holyhead in the next morning's near-storm, he watched white cobbled foam tumble over the rocks and comb away over their sides again. Ivy bush swung slack and jaunty underwater as dun-colored waves left trailing hoods of white when breaking on the beach. Called onto the ferry for Dublin, he stood at the railing in the wild air, his black felt hat in his hand and his coat sailing, imagining his five nuns nine years earlier, lamenting their exile from a haven that meant more to them than meat and drink.

•

University College was established by John Henry Newman to compete with Trinity College, Dublin, an esteemed and much richer Elizabethan foundation which would admit only Protestant students. Wedged into the upper stories of once-grand Georgian townhouses at 85 and 86 Stephen's Green, it was now, like Dublin, overcrowded, squalid, impoverished, and falling down, with filthy sanitation, crumbling plaster, hall doors that would not close, chipped ornamental flutes and festoons on the walls, and rotting draperies and valances. Rats inhabited all the drains and once were found in a stewpot. Ceiling paintings of gods and goddesses in what was once a luxurious salon were now painted over in chocolate brown so that the undergraduates in the make-do chapel would not be distracted by nudity. There were no laboratories for the science classes, and the sole libraries were those rows of books up and down the staircases that the instructors laid out from their own stock or bought from secondhand dealers by the sewer that was the River Liffey.

Dublin was a "joyless place," Hopkins wrote his friend Bridges, and of himself he wrote that "I am in a great weakness" and "I am, I believe, recovering from a deep fit of nervous prostration (I suppose I ought to call it): I did not know but I was dying."

"Black moods" and melancholia had troubled him all his life, but the bleakness increased in Dublin when he became the sole examiner of one paper each in Latin and Greek for the thousands who matriculated through the Royal University of Ireland. The sheer mass of papers would have been enough to tire most examiners or injure their eyes, but his conscientiousness made the correcting worse as he worked out a complex system of half- and quarter-marks for such things as misspellings and errors in tenses in order to ensure fairness and accuracy in his assessments. And the cultivation and refinement that Oxford sought to instill in its gentlemen were thought of as girlishness by his rough Irish undergraduates, and he was hurt to discover himself scorned, teased, and misinterpreted like some cartoon Englishman in need of tweaking.

In his manic phases, Hopkins took up horticulture and managed the greenhouse behind no. 86; he outlined a book on Homer's epic poetry and a book-long commentary on the *Spiritual Exercises*, of which only sketches survive; he became fascinated by John Stainer's *Theory of Harmony* and, though he could only play the piano with stabbing fingers, essayed a Gregorian score to accompany William Collins's "Ode to Evening."

And he could also claim much happiness in his Jesuit community, having found firm Irish friends in his Superior, Reverend William Delany, who was as "generous, cheering, and openhearted a man as I ever lived with," and in Mr. Robert Curtis, eight years his junior, a frail Jesuit mathematician whose epilepsy was an impediment to his ordination but who held the chair in Natural Sciences and was "my comfort beyond what I can say and a kind of godsend I never expected to have."

But there were increasing signs of psychological depression. Early rising was no longer easy for him, and he slogged through his workday as if he'd been sleepless. To his mother, he wrote, "I am going all to pieces with a cold," or "I am in a sort of languishing state of mind and body, but hobble on." Hopkins wrote Robert Bridges that his poetry was "at a standstill" and, in commenting on a publication of Canon Dixon's odes, interrupted himself to exclaim in capitals, "AND WHAT DOES ANYTHING AT ALL MATTER?"

His boyhood motto had been "To be rather than seem," but he reversed it in the first of the sonnets of desolation that would be the greatest poetic achievements of his Dublin years.

To seem the stranger lies my lot, my life
Among strangers. Father and mother dear,
Brothers and sisters are in Christ not near
And he my peace / my parting, sword and strife.

England, whose honour O all my heart woos, wife
To my creating thought, would neither hear
Me, were I pleading, plead nor do I: I wear-
Y of idle a being but by where wars are rife.

I am in Ireland now; now I am at a third
Remove. Not but in all removes I can
Kind love both give and get. Only what word

Wisest my heart breeds dark heaven's baffling ban
Bars or hell's spell thwarts. This to hoard unheard,
Heard unheeded, leaves me a lonely began.

•

One by one through the night, the iron lifeboats still with the *Deutschland* were torn off their davits and carried away.

A slaughter of wave caught a schoolboy and slammed him against the starboard railing. Hooked there by his clothing, he got his breath back as the sea slackened, but soon after that, a huge tonnage of wave raced into him again, crushing his right leg against the railing. When he fell free, blood was gushing from his thigh and he saw that his right leg was amputated and hanging by its trouser fabric from a pipe. The boy, Arnold Schwab, somehow survived.

A crew member seemed to hit his head on iron as he fell overboard, for though he came up swimming freestyle, he seemed unconscious of his objective, and while his friends called out, "This way! This way!" he swiveled around in the opposite direction and ducked under a hill of curling wave and did not rise up again.

Wilhelm Leick, of Cleveland, Ohio, took a lasso of rope with him as he clambered and shinnied his way up the rigging of the relatively unpopulated foremast, which many feared would topple like an axed tree from the continual jolts of the breakers. At the yardarm, Leick shoved the rope through his belt loops and wrapped it once more around his waist for security before tying himself to the upright mast. Seeing he still had a six-foot length of rope left, Theodor Teidemann joined him in his pillory up there where they watched children be required by the sea and noticed a still and patient man who just sat in truce with a concussion of wave and was covered by it and vanished.

Sixty feet above the confusion on the weather deck, Adolf Hermann was sitting on the bight of a rope, his high-top shoes underneath the shroud rope below, his left arm slung over a horizontal that braced his upper back while his right hung on to Anna Petzold's slim waist. She tilted into him as the ship teetered with the shocks of the waves, the sway of the mast at that height like the swoop of a playground swing.

"Are you cold, Anna?"

"Very."

"I have Scotch whisky for us."

"Whisky?"

"I stole it from the saloon," he said. "Because it's warming." She grinned at his dangerousness and daring as he tugged the glove off his left hand with his teeth. She took the glove from him as he got the Scotch from the side pocket of his mackinaw and chewed at the cork stopper in a fruitless effort to yank it out. Adolf finally resorted to striking the neck against an iron clevis until the cork and glass lip shattered off. Worried that shards of the flask might have infiltrated the whisky, he filled his own mouth first and swished the Scotch before he swallowed. With a squeezed voice, he said, "It's fine."

"And warming?"

"Like hot apple cider."

She opened her mouth as wide as a sparrow chick, and he was cautious with his pouring, but the ship swayed and she wiped her throat with her woolen scarf and said, "You're spilling it on my neck."

"Sorry." He tried again. "There?"

She winced. "Yes."

"How does it taste?"

"Like turpentine," she said. And coughed. But then she smiled. "Like *hot* turpentine. Thank you, Adolf."

High overhead a sailor aped his way across the yardarm and wildly jumped from strut to strut in the shrouds until he squatted just above them and said, "I have provisions for us if you'll give me some of that whisky." He reached inside his bulky peacoat and offered them his grocery of a loaf of black bread, a quarter-round of Tilsit cheese, and hackings of cold ham. "Eat, drink, and be merry," he said. "And everything that follows."

Adolf felt the riggings jiggling and glanced down at a man with a Vandyke beard and mustache laddering his way up. The grinning man, Richard something, hugged the ropes tight as he greeted them, his face near Adolf's high-top shoe. He waved off any whisky or food and introduced himself in a chatty, railroad compartment way, saying that he was originally from Switzerland but that he'd spent the last sixteen years in Shanghai. And just when Anna was inquiring what the Swiss man was doing in China, he lost hold of the ropes and with scared eyes fell backward, yelling unintelligibly as he tumbled and jounced down the rigging and smacked hard into the North Sea, where he died.

> They fought with God's cold—
> And they could not and fell to the deck
> (Crushed them) or water (and drowned them) or rolled
> With the sea-romp over the wreck.
> Night roared, with the heart-break hearing a heart-broke rabble,
> The woman's wailing, the crying of child without check—
> Till a lioness arose breasting the babble,
> A prophetess towered in the tumult, a virginal tongue told.

•

Hour after hour on the *Deutschland* there was screaming and yells for help that were so emotionally devastating for some that a stolid businessman named Waldheim took off his life vest and overcoat in the saloon and waded to his first-class cabin. But he was trailed by a suspicious stewardess who found him staring into his lavatory mirror, tears streaming down his face, and with a cocked derringer at his temple. She scolded, "We have so many ways to die here now. Why choose the only cowardly one?" And he put the derringer down.

Another man took off his striped tie and hanged himself from a joist of the pilothouse and was not noticed until his purple cheek mashed up against the aft window glass.

A child was lost at sea, and in order to join him in death his grieving mother sliced the veins of her wrists with a penknife.

The stewardess who convinced Waldheim not to commit suicide was headed to the pilothouse with an urn of coffee when she slipped on the ice of the weather deck and was purchased by a torrent of white, seething foam and was never seen again.

The ever-vigorous Carl Dietrich Meyer mountaineered his way up the rigging at Captain Brickenstein's first invitation, found a perch on the topmost yardarm of the mainmast, and tightly fastened himself to it. Even up as high as he was, the screams and shouts of injury were an agony to him, and he imagined these were the sounds of Hell, of chaos, helplessness, loss, sorrow, and sudden, perpetual loneliness. The ship had become an island of affliction and torture as a snowfield of sea foam washed over the quarterdeck, stealing whatever it could, and Meyer watched between his shroud-steadied shoes as the sea so angrily splashed up against the pilothouse that Captain Brickenstein and the crowd in there with him scurried out with the sea's next slackening and scrambled up onto the rigging.

A squalling child was left behind and was knocked flat by the sea. With the next swell, Carl Dietrich Meyer thought, she would be gone. But then a gymnastic seaman rappelled down the steep cliff of the rigging, as agile and unafraid as a chimpanzee, and he was just twenty feet above the little girl when his foot caught in a lanyard and he plummeted head-first. The sailor was secured to the yardarm by a legging, and in the sway of the mast he soared out over the sea upside down, and then gravity asked him back again in a glorious swing that ended when his neck struck a taut guy wire and his head was sliced off. The sea took the head as its own, but his body hung by its leg rope throughout the night, spilling blood and tolling the hours.

•

The flooding in the corridors was such that Second Officer Carl Thalenhorst could tilt forward to the saloon in the numbingly cold waist-high water only by yanking himself along on railings and doorframes and bolted-down furniture. And he was surprised to find more than twenty people still there on the islands of tables as a filthy lake of seawater, oil scum, and flotsam gradually rose around them, the sconced gaslights on the verge of going out. The saloon's aft was tilted higher, so most were crowding there. Children whined, there was intimacy among the married, a trinity of shivering steer-age passengers were involved in each other's overcoats for warmth. Closer, under the skylight, the Salzkotten nuns were reciting "The Litany of the Blessed Virgin Mary," the ghosts of their breath graying the air as Sister Barbara stated the many titles of Christ's mother, and the three others joined in the refrain, "Pray for us."

Thalenhorst noticed the little nun's teeth were chattering, and he called to Sister Barbara, "Won't you come topside?"

She shook her head.

Thalenhorst could no longer feel his feet; soon, he thought, a gangway heaped with luggage and mail bags would be too steep for him. And the hatches had been battened down. He struggled across the saloon, and the Salzkotten nuns stood up on the table as he swam onto it. Sister Barbara helped him stand and Thalenhorst unlatched the ice-rimed skylight and forced it open a little more than a foot. Colder sea air invaded the room.

Up on the weather deck, Dietrich Stege, the ship's carpenter, was hunched over in his peacoat and a stocking cap, holding up the skylight and interestedly staring down into the saloon.

"Help them out," Thalenhorst said.

But Sister Barbara said, "The children first."

Jacobine Schwartz, from Schweigen in Baden, slid down into the merciless cold of the water, and waded toward them, hefting up her five-year-old son so his head was higher than the flood. Thalenhorst hoisted Adam Schwartz up into Dietrich Stege's reaching hands, and the boy was yanked through the opening. And then Sister Barbara and Sister Norberta helped Thalenhorst lift Mrs. Schwartz. She scraped through the skylight with some effort, and Edward Stamm, carrying his Elise, waded over. He had to take his life vest off in order to wedge himself out, and then Thalenhorst lifted Elise to him.

But then there was another thundering shock and an inundation of seawater, and above them Jacobine Schwartz was shrieking for Adam, shrieking for help, shrieking that her child was overboard. And though Carl Thalenhorst swiftly climbed through the skylight to rescue the boy, the mother continued crying out for much too long, and then she distressingly howled in grief.

In spite of that tragedy, a young couple, with linked hands, risked going up. But they were the last.

Still with the Sisters in the dank saloon were a Czech family, three other women from steerage, and a baby girl who would not stop crying. Six tapers were found and lit and stuck in their wax to the highest shelves of the cabinets. Six ponds of yellow light.

An hour later Sister Norberta watched the Czech man's giant shadow lurch along the walls as he swashed through the saloon's belly-high lake to his wife with the dry woolen sweaters he'd scavenged held overhead. But he tripped against a submerged chair and toppled underwater. The Czech wife cried out when she saw him fall, and moaned in agony as he fought his way up again with cold, sodden sweaters that would do them no good. Her husband just stood there in the icy water, his shoulders jerking with sobs.

Sister Norberta told Sister Barbara, "I'm too cold to even shiver." Seeing Sister Brigitta holding tight a quiet Sister Aurea and gently rocking her sideways, Sister Norberta lost her shame and snuggled into the manly hug of Sister Barbara, whose wet cloak stank of salt water. Sister Norberta asked, "Why do you think God is doing this to us of all people? His devoted and adoring daughters?"

"His ways are not our ways," Sister Barbara stolidly stated.

"Is he punishing me for my sins? Am I being taught greater patience and humility?"

Sister Brigitta scoffed, "Such pride, Sister Norberta! A calamity affecting a hundred people and you think it's all because of you."

Sister Barbara said, "I have been picturing Mother Clara when she announced the government's war against us. She said only in Heaven will we understand the great mysteries of God's Providence."

"And what do you say?"

Sister Barbara thought for a minute. "We sometimes seem God's playthings. The dice he rolls. But even though he can seem the source of our miseries, our faith tells us that God is good. Always."

Sister Norberta said, "I have prayed for children to get well, and they did. I have prayed for children to get well, and they died."

"Well, prayer is not like money," Sister Brigitta said. "And Mother Clara used to say that God generally gives us something *better* than what we asked for."

Sister Barbara added, "I'm certain the Apostles prayed that Jesus would not be crucified. But he was."

"Such learning!" Sister Norberta said.

Sister Barbara ignored her.

Sister Aurea was losing consciousness, but she could still hear the Sisters talking. The fury of the sea was a continuous cannon, with the swells washing over the width of the ship with the growl of a wolf at the door. A children's story that scared her.

Sister Norberta's cheeks and mouth were stiffening and she ached everywhere. The seawater was rising higher than her ankles and she couldn't feel her feet. Would she lose them? Even her heart was sore. She felt so unwise, so under-educated. She wished Sister Henrica were here.

Sister Barbara softly shook her and warned, "Don't sleep."

I'm just resting, Sister Norberta wanted to say. She couldn't.

Sister Aurea could stand no longer and splashed to her knees on a tabletop that was now six inches underwater. Sister Barbara insisted she get up, but Sister Aurea answered non-sensically or in sentences no one could interpret because her speech was so slurred.

When Sister Brigitta held a taper light near the twenty-three-year-old's face, the widely dilated pupils would not shrink. Sister Brigitta took off a wet mitten and heated her right palm as well as she could with the candle flame before sliding a hand up inside Sister Aurea's sleeve. The skin was cold as marble, yet she wasn't shivering. She gripped Sister Aurea's wrist and counted a ragged pulse of fifty beats per minute. Sister Aurea was failing. Sister Brigitta remembered Dr. Damm telling the nurse the mathematics of threes: three weeks without food, three days without water, three hours without protection from the cold. And one dies.

Sister Aurea heard Sister Brigitta whisper something about a falling temperature to Sister Barbara, and Sister Aurea thought of herself as a girl in the kitchen and up on her toes, sticking a finger in a hot apple pie. *Josepha!* her mother scolded. *Josepha, what's gotten into you?* She was wearing a stained apron that she tripped over. Children used to laugh because Josepha Badziura wore hand-me-down clothes, and one time she fell in the classroom because she was wearing the too-big boots of a boy. She was so embarrassed she cried silently in the cloakroom.

Sister Brigitta was close as a memory now, and softly saying, "Sister Aurea? Shall we pray an Act of Contrition together?"

She couldn't recall the words. She was lying in a field making snow angels; no, she was on wood, and the rain was upside down. She wished it wasn't raining. She was so cold and wet everywhere. She was going to ruin her habit.

"O my God," Sister Brigitta recited. "I am heartily sorry for having offended thee."

And she went on saying things Sister Aurea couldn't understand, but it was like a sweet lullaby, a song urging a little one to sleep. And she was always such a good child. She slept.

Sister Mary Aurea Badziura, F.C.J.M. (1852–1875)

•

"She's gone," Sister Barbara said.

Sister Brigitta wiped tears from her cheeks and nodded a sullen acceptance.

"I meant Sister Norberta," Sister Barbara said.

She'd been silent for a while, and now Sister Norberta was lying with shut eyes against Sister Barbara's chest. Sister Brigitta couldn't recall ever seeing such a serenity of countenance in the woman. She'd been so hard on others. She'd seemed so cantankerous and unhappy, so little at peace. But this was how she looked when at rest. Lovable. Christ's bride.

"Cardiac arrest," Sister Barbara said. "Caused by hypothermia. Even the healthy die that way. And Sister Norberta was not well." Sister Barbara could be as tactless as a hammer.

"What was her name in the world?" Sister Brigitta asked.

"Johanna, I think."

Sister Brigitta was shivering as she dwelled on it. She tried to imagine Johanna Reinkober as a girl. It was impossible. She must have been old even as a child.

Sister Brigitta gave Sister Aurea's forehead a goodbye kiss and took off the life vest and forced the girl into a float. She inchingly turned on a current and was swallowed up into the night of the saloon.

Sister Barbara took off the life vest, let the stilled torso down, and slid the heavy body of Sister Norberta off the table. She placidly floated face up for a while and then gradually sank.

Sister Mary Norberta Reinkober, F.C.J.M. (1845–1875)

•

At three in the morning, the increasing north winds lowered the temperature to the dangerous, cruel, raw bitterness of winter, and toes and noses became frostbitten, even gloved hands lost their grip, and an exhausted Siegfried Benning could hang on no longer and skidded down into Anna Petzold and then flailed everywhere for a handhold in his long fall until he hit the sea face first.

Catharina Schlossbauer shawled herself in a tarpaulin and sat on the roof of the pilothouse, shying her eyes away from the headless seaman wavering upside down, still dripping blood, his noose on his ankle.

A man named Tylenda tried to waken the sister he'd tied to a mast for her safety and discovered she'd lost her life to exposure. Her torso and face like the stony statuary of agony, of bereavement.

The ship groaned in its overweight of water. An injured elephant noise.

August Lauenstein was up in the rigging next to the captain. Brickenstein's widened arms were hung over the ice-stiffened ropes as in a crucifixion. His head would dip forward in helpless sleep and then jerk up again, and Lauenstein reached out to clutch the captain's peacoat and hold him back from a fall.

Heymann Nathan could scan the shrouds above him and

in the silver moonlight count the inky shapes of one hundred twenty scared and shuddering crew members and passengers. Crows skeptically watching from trees.

Anna Petzold and Adolf Hermann squeezed together up there, their hands inside each other's shirts, and stayed awake by naming all the fine things they'd do or buy should they be rescued: hot cocoa in the Algonquin Hotel, a sheepskin coat and rabbit-fur gloves, a bath in scalding water. And then, after a silence, Adolf said, "But above all I would like to have you as my wife."

She seemed to be listening again to what he'd said. And then she rubbed her cold nose against his, like an Eskimo, and told him, "I do."

•

In the saloon the baby girl continued to cry insanely, but no one else was saying anything. In the eerie silence, Sister Brigitta wondered if they too had died.

"I have to help the baby," Sister Brigitta said.

Sister Barbara was silent. She was thinking of the science, that the human body loses heat to water thirty times faster than to the air. And the water would be heart high now.

Sister Brigitta gasped as she slipped into the shockingly icy flood and with hurt and difficulty surged toward the baby's noise, stroking in swim when the walk was too hard and sidestepping around Sister Aurea, who was shut-eyed just below the surface, her black veil wafting as softly as smoke over her white face.

Wind or wetness snuffed five of the six tapers, so that there was only a mist of yellow light in the gloom of the saloon. A hand seemed to be reaching to help Sister Brigitta up onto the furniture, but when she gripped it, she tugged the cold, dead woman over into seawater. Sister Brigitta sidled over to a mother sitting on an Austrian cherrywood bookcase, her head tilted to the side in death, but with her not-yet-year-old screaming baby girl buttoned inside the mother's otter coat and swaddled in a gray woolen scarf. Sister Brigitta could not get the child warmer than that, so she stood there in the cruelty of chest-high water, shushing the outrage and terror from the baby girl, and even singing a hymn she'd taught the orphans in Salzkotten.

Sister Barbara could hear Sister Brigitta singing, but the voice was soft and tremulous, and then silent. Even the baby was quiet. She could see no one. Was she alone here now? Sister Barbara could be self-sufficient and taciturn, masculine and pitiless, and some nuns presumed she was without emotion. But in truth emotions could so rule and overwhelm her that she'd learned to dam them up. *Cephas, Peter*, she thought, *was like that.* Contrary emotions spilling out of him whenever Jesus was around. Zeal and wonder, fear and shame. Wasn't she Peter now, seawater rising up and Thecla weakening so that she had to grip the iced iron frame of the skylight or sink to her death? "But when he saw the wind boisterous, he was afraid; and beginning to sink, he cried, saying, Lord, save me. And immediately Jesus stretched forth his hand." And now she needed Jesus to stretch forth his hand. Waiting for the end she was sure would be soon, she remembered verses from the Book of Revelation: "And the Spirit and the bride say, Come. And let him that heareth say, Come. And let him who is athirst come. And whosoever will, let him take the water of life freely." And she screamed into the night overhead, "O Christ, Christ come quickly!" But in their long ordeal on the *Deutschland*, she'd given up too much vitality, and she sank to her knees. "Even so, come, Lord Jesus," she said. Soon after that she died.

Sister Mary Barbara Hültenschmidt, F.C.J.M. (1843–1875)

•

But how shall I . . . make me room there:
Reach me a . . . Fancy, come faster—
Strike you the sight of it? look at it loom there,
Thing that she . . . there then! the Master,
Ipse, the only one, Christ, King, Head:
He was to cure the extremity where he had cast her;
Do, deal, lord it with living and dead;
Let him ride, her pride, in his triumph, despatch and have done with
his doom there.

•

Sister Brigitta was shored up by the bookcase and sleeping when she heard Sister Barbara scream to Christ. She wanted to shout back or wave, but couldn't. Her cheek was flat up against the mother's skirted thigh and she could rock her face away from it no more. With one eye she spied that the baby was now a stillborn, just a burden on the mother's belly. Sister Brigitta needed to pray for the dead, and so she recited in an interior way, "*Hail, Holy Queen, Mother of Mercy, our life, our sweetness, and our . . .*" Cold and weakness stole the ending and the next sentences but for *mourning and weeping in this vale of tears.* She was all but sleepwalking as she found a desk and senselessly sat at it as if she needed to pen a last will and testament. With frustration she went through the formula of the prayer again, but so much was missing and she was nearing unconsciousness. And then she happened upon the appeal *Turn, then, O most gracious Advocate, thine eyes of mercy toward us, and after this, our exile* . . . She reiterated *this, our exile.* Exiles from where? The prayer was meant for a world sour with sinning. Exiles, then, not from Germany, not from Europe, but from Paradise, from Heaven. And the others were no longer exiles. She slipped helplessly underwater, and joined them.

Sister Mary Brigitta Dammhorst, F.C.J.M. (1848–1875)

•

In a journal of his January 1889 retreat at the Saint Stanislaus Novitiate in Tullabeg, Hopkins examined his own "world without event" in Dublin and seemed to find no solace in it, for he recorded:

> What is my wretched life? Five wasted years have almost passed in Ireland. I am ashamed of the little I have done, of my waste of time, although my helplessness and weakness is such that I could scarcely do otherwise. And yet the Wise Man warns us against excusing ourselves in that fashion. I cannot then be excused; but what is life without aim, without spur, without help? All my undertakings miscarry: I am like a straining eunuch. I wish then for death: yet if I died now I should die imperfect, no master of myself, and that is the worst failure of all. O my God, look down on me.

•

Just before Easter, 1889, Francis de Paravicini, an old classmate who was on the Oxford faculty, visited Dublin and was staying at the Shelbourne Hotel. Because his evening was free, Paravicini strolled through the still-wintry park to no. 86 Stephen's Green in order to invite Hopkins out to dinner. An undergraduate hall porter left him outside in the cold as he stomped up the staircase to fetch the professor, and some minutes later a frail man in a worn cassock and ankle-high shoes was gingerly finding his way down the staircase, his hand squeakily gripping the banister. Elderly at forty-four. Without giving a reason, Hopkins graciously declined Paravicini's invitation out. Welts of insomnia pouched his eyes, and yet his white face was still boyish as he woozily crutched himself with the exterior door, his cheek weakly nestling against the cool, red-enameled wood as if fainting was a near-possibility. And when their conversation widened with silence, Hopkins said, "Oh, I'm so sorry to disappoint you. And so *sad*. Here you've come all this way."

Paravicini inquired, "Shall I be worried about you, Gerard?" And then he asked, "Why are you smiling?"

"I was just thinking of someone who calls me *Gerald*. How wonderful it is to be *known*."

"You appear so . . . distraught."

He smiled again. "But there you're wrong. I'm thoroughly and utterly straught."

"Is there anything I can do?"

Hopkins seemed to sink into an interior well, and then he said, "I just need some change, some relief."

When Paravicini got back to Oxford, he contacted the British Provincial and convinced Edwin Purbrick, he thought, to remove Hopkins from Ireland for his health. But Paravicini was told there would be a delay, that the majority of Jesuit reassignments were not announced until the Feast of Saint Ignatius on July 31st.

•

Imagine it otherwise. Imagine Hopkins being sent to Saint Beuno's to retrieve his strength in the "heavenfallen freshness" of Wales. Since he's there already, he joins the class of fourth-year theologians—still by no means the oldest of them—and becomes a Professed Father in 1890. And then he is assigned to Manresa House, in Roehampton, to teach Latin and Greek in the Juniorate. While there he publishes a collection of classical essays and a commentary on the *Spiritual Exercises* and becomes a much-sought-after spiritual director. As an editor of *The Month* preceding and during the Great War, he attracts England's finest writers to the journal through his conscientious criticisms and improvements, and one by one his Wales sonnets find their way into the journal's pages; "The Loss of the Eurydice" finds a home, so too "The Wreck of the Deutschland," the sonnets of desolation, and the stirring sonnets of consolation that followed them. In his old age he is sent to the newly founded Heythrop College, a Jesuit school of philosophy and theology at Oxford, and there he dies in 1929, the same year that Robert Bridges, the Poet Laureate of England, is featured on the cover of America's *Time* magazine.

•

The sea fell with ebb tide on December 7th and the winds calmed, and at sunrise those passengers and crew still up in the *Deutschland*'s rigging began gingerly climbing down. Some warmed their feet by tramping on the deck. Sails loosened by the storm were slapping in the breeze. Carl Dietrich Meyer numbered six dead women and one dead man still clinging with rigor mortis to wire gratings over the portholes on the leeward side of the ship, where waves washed over them through the night. Dietrich Stege got an oil can and started a fire that the coldest surrounded. Catharina Schlossbauer scavenged some food and laid it out on a tarpaulin.

At ten a.m., the English pilot Charles Dore Harvey spyglassed the shore of Harwich and viewed the paddle tugboat *Liverpool* steaming toward them. The nightmare was ending. The Harwich coast guard station had been telegraphed by officers of the naval barracks at Sheerness, where Quartermaster August Bock found landfall. Captained by John Carrington, the *Liverpool* reached the wreck a half hour later, moored alongside the *Deutschland* in three fathoms of sea, and rescued sixty-nine passengers, eighty-six crew, and the soggy mail sacks stacked in the gangways.

August Lauenstein counted heads and determined that forty-four passengers and twenty crew had died between five in the morning on December 6th and sunrise on December 7th.

A Cincinnati businessman risked a final descent into the saloon to get the contracts in his valise. He discovered eight women, a man, and two children were still there, dead. White-faced sisters in black veils and brown habits were floating in seawater. Sister Brigitta was sitting hunched at a desk, her head on her folded arms.

The captain reconnoitered his ship one last time, hunting official papers and a log book that were lost at sea, and he was the last of the living to leave the *Deutschland*, hopping onto a *Liverpool* that looked like an excursion boat with so many people jammed on its deck. Within days, there would be an inquest that was critical of Eduard Brickenstein for overrunning his course, but complimentary about his cautious actions after the ship struck the Kentish Knock. And yet he would never master a vessel again.

Those passengers who had survived the agonizing night in the pilothouse and rigging were ferried on the *Liverpool* to Harwich, where the Great Eastern Hotel hosted them. There a wife of a Member of Parliament presented each of them with nine shillings, and soon a public subscription raised one pound, seven shillings for each, as well as parcels of sundries for the journey still ahead and a parting gift of oranges.

Wreckers from the seaside towns raced their smacks out to the still-foundered *Deutschland* and rowdily swarmed through its holds and cabins, hurriedly looting it of jewelry, clothing, luggage, and valuables, then hauled off the piano, paintings, furniture, and cases of wine, and with claw hammers and crowbars deconstructed the dining hall and saloon just to get the sconces and fixtures. A pen-and-ink artist depicted the ugliness in *The Illustrated London News*, and editorials noted that such actions were not truly English.

Although corpses from the shipwreck continued to wash ashore over the next weeks, Sister Henrica Fassbender was never found. The other Salzkotten nuns were conveyed to the friary and Church of Saint Francis in Stratford, where their bodies were cleaned and their habits laundered by a girl named Mary Broadway, who herself would become a Poor Clare. Laid out in elmwood coffins in the school hall below the church, Sisters Barbara, Norberta, Brigitta, and Aurea were surrounded by a grand abundance of flowers and wreaths, and were visited by sizable crowds of Protestants and Catholics. Their solemn Requiem Mass on December 11th was attended by no less than fifty priests, and His Eminence Cardinal Henry Edward Manning preached an emo-

tional and political oration linking the deaths of the Salzkotten nuns to the persecutions of the Catholic Church in Germany. The nuns were buried in Saint Patrick's Cemetery at
Leytonstone, a village adjacent to the one where Gerard
Manley Hopkins was born.

•

On April 29th, 1889, Hopkins sent the sonnet "To R.B." to
his "Dearest Bridges." Shakespearean in tone, stately in its
pace, the poem likened inspiration to "The fine delight that
fathers thought; the strong / Spur, live and lancing like the
blowpipe flame." On May 1st Hopkins wrote his mother that
he ought to have been preparing the Royal University of
Ireland examinations in classics but was inconvenienced by
what he thought was rheumatic fever. On May 3rd he wrote
his father that he was laid out with that illness. Alluding to a
then popular and sentimental melody, he wished that the
songwriters "would agree to plant a garden, a garden of sleep
in my bed, as I am sleepy by day and sleepless by night and do
not rightly sleep at all." Dr. Redmond, he told his father, diag-
nosed his illness to be the result of a flea bite and had instituted
"a treatment which begets confidence but not gratitude."

On May 4th, Reverend Thomas Wheeler, the forty-year-
old vice-president of University College and minister of the
house, noticed that Hopkins had not made it to the Jesuit dining room for breakfast and found him still in his bed, hotly
fevered and racked with intestinal pain. A Dublin nurse was
summoned from Saint Vincent's Hospital to embarrass him
with an enema. On May 5th, a Sunday, Hopkins was upright long enough to say a private Mass, which helped his
spirits, and to pen a pacifying letter to his mother in which he
noted:

It is an ill wind that blows nobody good. My sickness falling
at the most pressing time of the University work, there will
be the devil to pay. Only there is no harm in saying, that gives
me no trouble but an unlooked for relief. At many such a time
I have been in a sort of extremity of mind, now I am the
placidest soul in the world. And you will see, when I come
round, I shall be the better for this.

Still, Kate Hopkins was in a panic over her eldest son's
health and sent him a red and yellow bouquet of gerberas,
tiger lilies, and carnations that slowly revived in the porcelain
vase on his side table. Hopkins hoped to sit up to send a reply of gratitude but could not, and so, on May 8th, Tom
Wheeler hunched over Hopkins's stand-up writing desk and
took down a dictation in which Hopkins told his mother his
illness was a sort of typhoid, but not severe. He was still alert.
He said he had tried to ease his head fever with the cooling
winds outdoors, but only managed to contract a case of neu-
ralgia. The nursing was excellent, he claimed, and hot beef
tea, chicken jelly, and medicines "keep coming in like cricket
balls. I have in fact every attention possible. Best love to all—
Your affectionate son GERARD."

The minister folded the page into an envelope and ad-
dressed it according to Hopkins's instructions. And because
there still was time before the postman came, Wheeler asked,
"Would you like to hear the Office?"

"Yes."

Wheeler ribboned Hopkins's breviary for the readings of
May 8th and crossed his mouth with his thumb as he recited
in Latin, "Lord, open my lips."

Hopkins shut his eyes for the antiphon: "And my mouth
shall proclaim your praise."

•

Because there were fears that others in the Jesuit cloister might be infected by such a communicable disease, Hopkins was shifted from no. 86 to a larger, sunnier hospital room on the ground floor of no. 85 Stephen's Green. Six days later, Reverend Wheeler sent a note to Mrs. Hopkins saying, "You will be glad to hear that he is still keeping up his strength admirably and if I, a non-professional, may judge, I think he is now well round the corner and on the high road to mending." Wheeler also sent a note to Robert Bridges, who replied on May 18th, 1889, from his country estate of Yattendon:

Dearest Gerard,

I am sorry to get a letter from one of your people telling me that you were ill with fever. And yesterday I sent you off a budget of notes on Milton's prosody. And when I last wrote I never mentioned your ailing though you told me in your letter that you interrupted it to lie down. What is this fever? Fr. Wheeler says that you are mending. I hope that you are recovering properly. Let me have a line. I wish I could look in on you and see for myself.

You must send me a card now and then, and one as soon as possible to let me know about you.

Meanwhile I must be patient. I think that if you are really mending, Miltonic prosody will be just the sort of light amusement for your mind. I hope you are well enough already. And will make a quiet recovery and complete for which I pray. Your affectionate,

RB

•

The chaos of oceans in a headache like no other, a roaring in his ears as the great dragon waves stack up high, and then the cataclysm, the noise like lightning sketching across a night sky and then cannoning. And he lies helpless, still, his mind in a swim. *I am soft sift / In an hourglass.* Hearing good Tom Wheeler is there, he tries to lift a hand in hello, but cannot. A nurse is whispering instructions about acute peritonitis. But he is shipwrecked and foundered, the prey of the gales. A cold washrag paints his face, is folded onto his forehead, but he cannot look in time to see whose hand. The contrariness of the body: to be chilled with fever. Hearing the nurse's word "enteric," he thinks from the Greek *enterikós,* the Latin *intrare,* to enter, but derived from *intra,* within. And so, lads, intestinal. And typhoid? Also Greek, from *typhos,* vapor— for contaminated air? Or was he contaminated by food or water, Dublin itself? Was he the contaminant? *But how shall I . . . make me room there: / Reach me a . . . Fancy, come faster—Strike you the sight of it? look at it loom there, / Thing that she . . . there then! the Master—*

"No need to keep it secret," said the nurse in a hush.

Wheeler asked, "Would *you* want to know?"

"I would, oh indeed," said the nurse.

And the house minister's voice, overloud, as with the aged. "Gerard? Are you wakeful?"

There was an aching in his neck as he could just once and gradually nod his head, his eyes tightly closed from the crash of sunlight.

"I'm afraid you have taken a serious turn for the worse. I have summoned your father and mother."

"How nice," Hopkins said, and then found the reserves to try a full sentence. "I shall be glad to see them."

•

Jesuit faculty visited him. Reverend Carbery, who'd replaced William Delany as University College president, read aloud some of Thomas Babington Macaulay's *History of England* to him, and on shutting the book vouchsafed his opinion that Macaulay wrote livelier prose than even John Henry Newman.

Even in his illness, Hopkins's literary criticisms were uncensored, and he parried: "You might as well say that *Punch* is livelier than the Bible."

"*Touché,*" Carbery said.

The French Jesuit Père Mallac exhibited his gallery of photographs to the man he called "Zherr-y," one of them an excellent portrait of Hopkins captured while he was strolling.

Reverend Matthew Russell, the editor of *The Irish Monthly*, had published two of Hopkins's Latin versions of Shakespeare's songs and bucked up his spirits by hoping Hopkins would contribute another soon.

Reverend Tom Finlay heard his confession, and included in it was Hopkins's confession not just of sins such as petulance, laziness, and rash judgment but of shutting off the grace of inspiration by not paying enough attention to his poetic gift.

The confessor stared with confusion. "I didn't know you wrote poetry."

"I don't," Hopkins said, "but I did once." And then he looked away.

Robert Curtis stayed with him when Tom Wheeler could not and stood at the foot of his bed as he told him, "I have always been edified by your priestly spirit, Gerard. It's not just the reverence with which you say Mass or speak on sacred subjects, but your whole conduct and conversation. And your devotion and loyalty to the Society. Edifying in the extreme."

"Thank you."

"Remember our holiday together in Wales? 'The Arcadia of wild beauty,' you called it."

He smiled in reminiscence. "Waterfalls. Climbing Mount Snowdon."

"And my parents always so enjoyed your company."

"And I them." Emotion silenced Curtis, and Hopkins saw it. "I shall sleep now," he said.

•

The faces of friends and relatives who had died visited him continually in his dreams, each smiling and welcoming. Well dressed, in a grand ballroom, with an orchestra playing Henry Purcell. And five nuns, off to the side so he could not see their faces. He felt a thumb form a cross on his forehead and smelled the olive oil of anointing. Extreme unction. Sentences were being recited in Latin, but he could not make them out. Soon, he knew, he would be given Communion, *viaticum*, to have Christ with him on the journey. He was sinking into the lake of unconsciousness when he heard Wheeler say in English, "Gerard? Will you please open your eyes?"

He did. The house minister was wearing a purple stole over his cassock. Six or more solemn Jesuits crowded the room. Wheeler held out a Host and recited, *"Corpus Dómini nostri Jesu Christi custódiat ánimam tuam in vitam ætérnam."*

Hopkins said, "Amen," and took the round white wafer on his tongue, then shut his eyes again for his post-Communion prayers. But instead he recalled his own final lines from "The Wreck of the Deutschland":

> Dame, at our door
>   Drowned, and among our shoals,
>   Remember us in the roads, the heaven-haven of the Reward:
>   Our King back, oh, upon English souls!
> Let him easter in us, be a dayspring to the dimness of us, be a
>   crimson-cresseted east,
>   More brightening her, rare-dear Britain, as his reign rolls,
>   Pride, rose, prince, hero of us, high-priest,
> Our hearts' charity's hearth's fire, our thoughts' chivalry's throng's Lord.

•

Curtis escorted Manley and Kate Hopkins into the ground-floor room in the late morning that Saturday, June 8th. Emaciated and as white as his sheets, he seemed already dead, but when his mother shrieked and fell to her knees next to him, she jostled the bed and the lancing pain in his abdomen woke him. She kissed his face and keened over him, and then his head rolled to see his father. Smiling, he joked, *"Ave atque vale,"* a signature line from Cicero: Hail and farewell.

"A first for us," his father said. "Seeing you in your digs."

"I shall have to give you a tour."

Wheeler brought in a dining-room chair, and Manley Hopkins helped his wife onto it and formally stood beside her in his fine banker's suit, a hand on her scarfed shoulder as she questioned her son about his illness and his medicines.

But his thoughts were elsewhere. "I have lost interest in

myself," he said, and closed his eyes and slipped into unconsciousness.

His mother petted his ginger-brown hair with her hand. She said with tears, "Don't you think he looks handsome?"

His father was without sentences.

Curtis carried down some pencil drawings of nature scenes from Hopkins's room, of hornbeams, scrolled ash, chance-quarried rocks. His father stared at them in silence. "There's also some of his writing upstairs," Curtis said, and his father nodded.

The house minister carried in sliced lemons and a porcelain tea service to help them in their watch.

Hopkins whispered, and his mother tilted forward to hear him saying, "I'm so happy. I'm so happy."

And then, at half past one in the afternoon, he died.

Epilogue

P O E M S

The funeral was held on Tuesday, June 11th, in the Jesuit church on Upper Gardiner Street, and a significant procession took him to Prospect Cemetery in Glasnevin, where Irish Jesuits are interred. And there Pater Gerardus Hopkins was buried, like his exiled nuns, in a country not his own.

Writing of his death to a mutual friend, Robert Bridges stated, "That dear Gerard was overworked, unhappy & would never have done anything great seems to give no solace. But how much worse it wd have been had his promise or performance been more splendid. He seems to have been entirely lost & destroyed by those Jesuits."

Robert Bridges's mother was gentler, writing to Mrs. Kate Hopkins, "I looked upon him always as a Holy Spiritual, more than an Earthly Being, and I loved to know and feel he was Robert's real friend."

Although the Society of Jesus technically controlled the rights to Hopkins's poetry, Bridges was allowed to act as his literary executor, and in August 1889, Bridges announced his plan to have some of his friend's verse and a memoir of him by Richard Watson Dixon printed by the chapbook publisher

C.H.O. Daniel. But Canon Dixon was old and not up to the task, and Dr. Bridges's own conservative scruples over revealing even the most innocent intimacies in their private correspondence, coupled with worries that the general public would find the poetry freakish and obscure, caused him to stall on the project. And given the opportunity to select some of his friend's poems for the anthology *The Poets and the Poetry of the Century*, he struggled to find anything good to say:

> His early verse shows a mastery of Keatsian sweetness, but he soon developed a very different style of his own, so full of experiments in rhythm and diction that were his poems collected into one volume, they would appear as a unique effort in English literature. Most of his poems are religious, and marked with Catholic theology, and almost all are injured by a natural eccentricity, a love for subtlety and uncommonness . . . And this quality of mind hampered their author throughout life; for though to a fine intellect and varied accomplishments . . . he united humor, great personal charm, and the most attractive virtues of a tender and sympathetic nature—which won him love wherever he went, and gave him zeal for his work— yet he was not considered publicly successful in his profession.

An undelighted reviewer for the Manchester *Guardian* confirmed Bridges's negative opinion of the eccentricities, noting: "Curiosities like the verses of the late Gerard Hopkins should be excluded." But gradually other anthologies began including a poem or two, and in 1909 the magazine *Catholic World* published Katherine Brégy's "Gerard Hopkins: An Epitaph and Appreciation." Bridges sent the essay to Mrs. Hopkins with the resistant, dismissive, envious note:

"The Catholics are very hard up for any literary interests, and are glad enough to make something of Gerard's work." And when, five months later, the English Jesuit Joseph Keating sought to use Hopkins's poems in a series of articles, Bridges was again obstructive, writing to Mrs. Hopkins: "I do not think Gerard wd have wished his poems to be edited by a committee of those fellows," and "I am sure they wd make a dreadful mess of the whole thing."

English literature owes Robert Bridges a great debt for his copying of the handwritten poems into a blank book as he got them, for Hopkins himself was notoriously casual about their preservation. But Bridges at first seemed to consider the poems the outlandish experiments of a crude amateur and was never wholly at ease with his friend's work. Even in his editorial notes in the collected *Poems* of 1918—which he titled identically to his own first book—Bridges could not forgive his friend's licenses:

> Apart from questions of taste—and if these poems were to be arraigned for errors of what may be called taste, they might be convicted of occasional affectation in metaphor . . . or of some perversion of human feeling . . . [T]hese and a few such examples are mostly efforts to force emotion into theological or sectarian channels . . . or, again, [there is] the exaggerated Marianism of some pieces, or the naked encounter of sensualism and asceticism.

Bridges disliked "all the rude shocks of his purely artistic wantonness," "definite faults of style which a reader must have courage to face," and a disconcerting lack of "literary decorum." Reading Bridges's notes on Hopkins's poems in

1920, an American reviewer in *Poetry* exclaimed, "From our best friends, deliver us, O Lord!"

Kate Hopkins would live to the age of ninety-eight—a half-century longer than her firstborn son—and she wept when she saw that the collection was dedicated to her. Oxford University Press initially printed 750 copies of *Poems* and it took twelve years for that first edition to sell out. But even when in its second year of publication the book sold a third more copies than in its first, Bridges scoffed, "Truly the world is upside down—and its rump is not altogether beautiful."

Robert Bridges was the grand man of English letters then, since 1913 the Poet Laureate, and he could not have foreseen how interest in his own poetry would languish just as interest in Gerard Manley Hopkins's grew. A second edition of the book with additional poems and a critical introduction by Charles Williams and now titled *Poems of Gerard Manley Hopkins* was published by Oxford in 1930, and important critics such as I. A. Richards, Laura Riding, Robert Graves, and William Empson were closely analyzing Hopkins's innovations as precursors to Modernism. As early as 1932, the great British literary critic F. R. Leavis could write that Hopkins "is likely to prove, for our time and the future, the only influential poet of the Victorian age, and he seems to me the greatest."

In April 1930, his eighty-fifth year, Robert Bridges died at Boar's Hill, Oxford. He was handsome to the end: his obituary in *The* (London) *Times* mentioned his "great stature and fine proportions, his leonine head, deep eyes, expressive lips, and a full-toned voice, made more effective by a slight, occasional hesitation in his speech." And so Bridges was used to fawning admiration when some months earlier he was visited by the British novelists Virginia Woolf and Aldous Huxley. Like a praying mantis, the anorexic young Huxley folded himself into a sunroom armchair and owlishly scanned in silence Bridges's most popular collection, *The Testament of Beauty*. But Woolf gently sought her host's scrapbook of the handwritten poems by Hopkins. White-haired Bridges indulged the lovely woman and achingly sat into what he'd nicknamed his "Victrola chair" in the music room, heating his joints with a Scotch-plaid blanket as he watched with gall and wormwood as the interesting author of *Night and Day* and *To the Lighthouse* marveled over the exacting vocabulary and imagery of his Oxford classmate, now forty years gone.

And he journeyed back to the 1870s and a late afternoon such as this in his London home on Bedford Square. There had been some feast of Catholic piety that Hopkins was obliged to attend, and so he was still in his priest's clothing when he arrived, but he was otherwise the peppy Gerard he'd first met at the Sunday night "Tea, Toast, and Testament" in 1863: small, insouciant, incisive, certain in his convictions. Dr. Bridges had gone into his kitchen to fetch a whisky from the Isle of Islay, and when he got back he found Hopkins holding like a sacrament Bridges's *Poems*, turning each page with the care of a learned botanist scrutinizing an unclassified leaf. His examination was quiet, deliberate, exhaustive; it seemed not so much reading as it was fathoming, seeing deep into the soul of each poem. And when he had dipped into the book in several places, Hopkins glanced up at his friend and grinned. "I say, what fun, Bridges, if you were to be a classic!"

Which in turn reminded the ailing Bridges of how touched and graced with misgivings he was when the Jesuits

APPENDIX

A NOTE ON SOURCES

APPENDIX

THE WRECK OF THE DEUTSCHLAND

*To the
happy memory of five Franciscan Nuns
exiles by the Falk Laws
drowned between midnight and morning of
Dec. 7th, 1875*

PART THE FIRST

1

    Thou mastering me
      God! giver of breath and bread;
   World's strand, sway of the sea;
      Lord of living and dead;
Thou hast bound bones and veins in me, fastened me flesh,
And after it almost unmade, what with dread,
     Thy doing: and dost thou touch me afresh?
Over again I feel thy finger and find thee.

2

    I did say yes
      O at lightning and lashed rod;
   Thou heardst me truer than tongue confess
      Thy terror, O Christ, O God;
Thou knowest the walls, altar and hour and night:
The swoon of a heart that the sweep and the hurl of thee trod
     Hard down with a horror of height:
And the midriff astrain with leaning of, laced with fire of stress.

3

The frown of his face
Before me, the hurtle of hell
Behind, where, where was a, where was a place?
I whirled out wings that spell
And fled with a fling of the heart to the heart of the Host.
My heart, but you were dovewinged, I can tell,
Carrier-witted, I am bold to boast,
To flash from the flame to the flame then, tower from the grace to the
grace.

4

I am soft sift
In an hourglass—as the wall
Fast, but mined with a motion, a drift,
And it crowds and it combs to the fall;
I steady as a water in a well, to a poise, to a pane,
But roped with, always, all the way down from the tall
Fells or flanks of the voel, a vein
Of the gospel proffer, a pressure, a principle, Christ's gift.

5

I kiss my hand
To the stars, lovely-asunder
Starlight, wafting him out of it; and
Glow, glory in thunder;
Kiss my hand to the dappled-with-damson west;
Since, tho' he is under the world's splendour and wonder,
His mystery must be instressed, stressed;
For I greet him the days I meet him, and bless when I understand.

6

Nor out of his bliss
Springs the stress felt
Nor first from heaven (and few know this)
Swings the stroke dealt—
Stroke and a stress that stars and storms deliver,
That guilt is hushed by, hearts are flushed by and melt—
But it rides time like riding a river
(And here the faithful waver, the faithless fable and miss).

7

It dates from the day
Of his going in Galilee;
Warm-laid grave of a womb-life grey;
Manger, maiden's knee;
The dense and the driven Passion, and frightful sweat;
Thence the discharge of it, there its swelling to be,
Though felt before, though in high flood yet—
What none would have known of it, only the heart, being hard
at bay,

8

Is out with it! Oh,
We lash with the best or worst
Word last! How a lush-kept plush-capped sloe
Will, mouthed to flesh-burst,
Gush!—flush the man, the being with it, sour or sweet,
Brim, in a flash, full!—Hither then, last or first,
To hero of Calvary, Christ's feet—
Never ask if meaning it, wanting it, warned of it—men go.

9

Be adored among men,
God, three-numberèd form;
Wring thy rebel, dogged in den,
Man's malice, with wrecking and storm.
Beyond saying sweet, past telling of tongue,
Thou art lightning and love, I found it, a winter and warm;
Father and fondler of heart thou has wrung:
Hast thy dark descending and most art merciful then.

10

With an anvil-ding
And with fire in him forge thy will
Or rather, rather then, stealing as Spring
Through him, melt him but master him still:
Whether at once, as once at a crash Paul,
Or as Austin, a lingering-out sweet skill,
Make mercy in all of us, out of us all
Mastery, but be adored, but be adored King.

PART THE SECOND

I I

'Some find me a sword; some
The flange and the rail; flame,
Fang, or flood' goes Death on drum,
And storms bugle in his fame.
But we dream we are rooted in earth—Dust!
Flesh falls within sight of us, we, though our flower the same,
Wave with the meadow, forget that there must
The sour scythe cringe, and the blear share come.

I 2

On Saturday sailed from Bremen,
American-outward-bound,
Take settler and seamen, tell men with women,
Two hundred souls in the round—
O Father, not under thy feathers nor ever as guessing
The goal was a shoal, of a fourth the doom to be drowned;
Yet did the dark side of the bay of thy blessing
Not vault them, the millions of rounds of thy mercy not reeve even
them in?

I 3

Into the snows she sweeps,
Hurling the haven behind,
The Deutschland, on Sunday; and so the sky keeps,
For the infinite air is unkind,
And the sea flint-flake, black-backed in the regular blow,
Sitting Eastnortheast, in cursed quarter, the wind;
Wiry and white-fiery and whirlwind-swivellèd snow
Spins to the widow-making unchilding unfathering deeps.

I 4

She drove in the dark to leeward,
She struck—not a reef or a rock
But the combs of a smother of sand: night drew her
Dead to the Kentish Knock;
And she beat the bank down with her bows and the ride of her keel:
The breakers rolled on her beam with ruinous shock;

And canvas and compass, the whorl and the wheel
Idle for ever to waft her or wind her with, these she endured.

1 5
Hope had grown grey hairs,
Hope had mourning on,
Trenched with tears, carved with cares,
Hope was twelve hours gone;
And frightful a nightfall folded rueful a day
Nor rescue, only rocket and lightship, shone,
And lives at last were washing away:
To the shrouds they took,—they shook in the hurling and horrible airs.

1 6
One stirred from the rigging to save
The wild woman-kind below,
With a rope's end round the man, handy and brave—
He was pitched to his death at a blow,
For all his dreadnought breast and braids of thew:
They could tell him for hours, dandled the to and fro
Through the cobbled foam-fleece, what could he do
With the burl of the fountains of air, buck and the flood of the wave?

1 7
They fought with God's cold—
And they could not and fell to the deck
(Crushed them) or water (and drowned them) or rolled
With the sea-romp over the wreck.
Night roared, with the heart-break hearing a heart-broke rabble,
The woman's wailing, the crying of a child without check—
Till a lioness arose breasting the babble,
A prophetess towered in the tumult, a virginal tongue told.

1 8
Ah, touched in your bower of bone
Are you! turned for an exquisite smart,
Have you! make words break from me here all alone,
Do you!—mother of being in me, heart.
O unteachably after evil, but uttering truth,
Why, tears! is it? tears; such a melting, a madrigal start!

Never-eldering revel and river of youth,
What can it be, this glee? the good you have there of your own?

19

    Sister, a sister calling
    A master, her master and mine!—
  And the inboard seas run swirling and hawling;
    The rash smart sloggering brine
Blinds her; but she that weather sees one thing, one;
Has one fetch in her: she rears herself to divine
    Ears, and the call of the tall nun
To the men in the tops and the tackle rode over the storm's brawling.

20

    She was first of a five and came
    Of a coifèd sisterhood.
  (O Deutschland, double a desperate name!
    O world wide of its good!
But Gertrude, lily, and Luther, are two of a town,
  Christ's lily and beast of the waste wood:
    From life's dawn it is drawn down,
Abel is Cain's brother and breasts they have sucked the same.)

21

    Loathed for a love men knew in them,
    Banned by the land of their birth,
  Rhine refused them. Thames would ruin them;
    Surf, snow, river and earth
Gnashed: but thou art above, thou Orion of light;
Thy unchancelling poising palms were weighing the worth,
    Thou martyr-master: in thy sight
Storm flakes were scrolled-leaved flowers, lily showers—sweet heaven
    was astrew in them.

22

    Five! the finding and sake
    And cipher of suffering Christ.
  Mark, the mark is of man's make
    And the word of it Sacrificed.
But he scores it in scarlet himself on his own bespoken,

Before-time-taken, dearest prizèd and priced—
    Stigma, signal, cinquefoil token
For lettering of the lamb's fleece, ruddying of the rose-flake.

23

    Joy fall to thee, father Francis,
      Drawn to the Life that died;
    With the gnarls of the nails in thee, niche of the lance, his
      Lovescape crucified
And seal of his seraph-arrival! and these thy daughters
    And five-livèd and leavèd favour and pride,
      Are sisterly sealed in wild waters,
To bathe in his fall-gold mercies, to breath in his all-fire glances.

24

    Away in the loveable west,
      On a pastoral forehead of Wales,
    I was under a roof here, I was at rest,
      And they the prey of the gales;
She to the black-about air, to the breaker, the thickly
    Falling flakes, to the throng that catches and quails
      Was calling 'O Christ, Christ, come quickly':
The cross to her she calls Christ to her, christens her wild-worst Best.

25

    The majesty! what did she mean?
      Breathe, arch and original Breath.
    Is it love in her of the being as her lover had been?
      Breathe, body of lovely Death.
They were else-minded then, altogether, the men
    Woke thee with a *we are perishing* in the weather of Gennesareth.
      Or is it that she cried for the crown then,
The keener to come at the comfort for feeling the combating keen?

26

    For how to the heart's cheering
      The down-dugged ground-hugged grey
    Hovers off, the jay-blue heavens appearing
      Of pied and peeled May!
Blue-beating and hoary-glow height: or night, still higher,

With belled fire and the moth-soft Milky Way,
  What by *your* measure is the heaven of desire,
The treasure never eyesight got, nor was ever guessed what for the
  hearing?

27

    No, but it was not these,
    The jading and jar of the cart,
  Time's tasking, it is fathers that asking for ease
  Of the sodden-with-its-sorrowing heart,
Not danger, electrical horror; then further it finds
The appealing of the Passion is tenderer in prayer apart:
  Other, I gather, in measure her mind's
Burden, in wind's burly and beat of endragonèd seas.

28

    But how shall I . . . make me room there:
    Reach me a . . . Fancy, come faster—
  Strike you the sight of it? look at it loom there,
    Thing that she . . . there then! the Master,
Ipse, the only one, Christ, King, Head:
He was to cure the extremity where he had cast her;
  Do, deal, lord it with living and dead;
Let him ride, her pride, in his triumph, despatch and have done with
  his doom there.

29

    Ah! there was a heart right!
    There was single eye!
  Read the unshapeable shock night
    And knew the who and the why;
Wording it how but by him that present and past,
Heaven and earth are word of, worded by?—
  The Simon Peter of a soul! to the blast
Tarpeian-fast, but a blown beacon of light.

30

    Jesu, heart's light,
    Jesu, maid's son,
  What was the feast followed the night
    Thou hadst glory of this nun?—

Feast of the one woman without stain.
For so conceivèd, so to conceive thee is done;
   But here was heart-throe, birth of a brain,
Word, that heard and kept thee and uttered thee outright.

3 1
   Well, she has thee for the pain, for the
    Patience; but pity of the rest of them!
   Heart, go and bleed at a bitterer vein for the
    Comfortless unconfessed of them—
No not uncomforted: lovely-felicitous Providence
Finger of a tender of, O of a feathery delicacy, the breast of the
   Maiden could obey so, be a bell to, ring of it, and
Startle the poor sheep back! is the shipwrack then a harvest, does
   tempest carry the grain for thee?

3 2
   I admire thee, master of the tides,
    Of the Yore-flood, of the year's fall;
   The recurb and the recovery of the gulf's sides,
    The girth of it and the wharf of it and the wall;
Stanching, quenching ocean of a motionable mind;
Ground of being, and granite of it: past all
   Grasp God, throned behind
Death with a sovereignty that heeds but hides, bodes but
   abides;

3 3
   With a mercy that outrides
    The all of water, an ark
   For the listener; for the lingerer with a love glides
    Lower than death and the dark;
A vein for the visiting of the past-prayer, pent in prison,
The-last-breath penitent spirits—the uttermost mark
   Our passion-plungèd giant risen,
The Christ of the Father compassionate, fetched in the storm of his
   strides.

3 4
   Now burn, new born to the world,
    Doubled-naturèd name,

The heaven-flung, heart-fleshed, maiden-furled
   Miracle-in-Mary-of-flame,
Mid-numbered He in three of the thunder-throne!
Not a dooms-day dazzle in his coming nor dark as he came;
   Kind, but royally reclaiming his own;
A released shower, let flash to the shire, not a lightning of fire
   hard-hurled.

35

   Dame, at our door
   Drowned, and among our shoals,
Remember us in the roads, the heaven-haven of the Reward:
   Our King back, oh, upon English souls!
Let him easter in us, be a dayspring to the dimness of us, be a
   crimson-cresseted east,
More brightening her, rare-dear Britain, as his reign rolls,
   Pride, rose, prince, hero of us, high-priest,
Our hearts' charity's hearth's fire, our thoughts' chivalry's throng's
   Lord.

Regrettably, very little is known about the five Sisters who drowned in the shipwreck of the *Deutschland* in 1875. The historical information that provided the basis for my fictional interpretation is primarily based on accounts in *The Times* of London, Sean Street's 1992 investigation *The Wreck of the Deutschland*, and *The Floundering Rescue* by Reverend Michael Klaus Wernicke, O.S.A., which was translated from the German by Sister Audrey Marie Rothweil, F.C.J.M., who gave me invaluable help on this project soon after I began it.

A great deal more is known about Reverend Gerard M. Hopkins, S.J., thanks to the ever-increasing interest in his life and works. I have profited by a wide variety of books and articles about him, but of particular value to me were *The Great Sacrifice* by David Downes; *Canute's Tower, St. Beuno's* by Paul Edwards, S.J.; *A Commentary on the Complete Poems of Gerard Manley Hopkins* by Paul Mariani; *A Commentary on G. M. Hopkins' The Wreck of the Deutschland* by Peter Milward, S.J.; *Gerard Manley Hopkins: The Wreck of the Deutschland* by Leo Martin van Noppen; *Gerard Manley Hopkins: A Critical Edition of the Major Works*, edited by Catherine Phillips; *Hopkins the Jesuit: The Years of Training* by Alfred Thomas, S.J.; and Norman White's three major biographical studies: *Hopkins: A Literary Biography, Gerard Manley Hopkins in Wales,* and *Hopkins in Ireland.*

Mick McCarthy, S.J., helped me with the Latin I confronted in my researches, and Gerry McKevitt, S.J., with the ways of the Society of Jesus in the nineteenth century. Early on, William Rewak, S.J., gifted me with *The Correspondence of Gerard Manley Hopkins and Richard Watson Dixon* and *The Notebooks and Papers of Gerard Manley Hopkins.* Stephanie Edwards Plowman, curator of the Anthony Bischoff S.J. Research Collection at Gonzaga University, provided quick responses to my questions. And I must again express my thanks to Richard and Elizabeth Moley for funding the endowed professorship in Hopkins's name that has given me time to continue writing. Also of financial assistance early on was a Thomas Terry Research Grant, a research fellowship from the Bannan Center for Jesuit Education, and three quarters of sabbatical leave, all from Santa Clara University.

Joseph Feeney, S.J., is perhaps the dean of Hopkins studies and is co-editor of *The Hopkins Quarterly.* Whenever I had a question, I needed only to shoot an e-mail to him, and he would send back an apt and supportive reply. The same holds true for my old friend Paul Mariani. It was my great good fortune that he was writing his definitive biography of Hopkins just as I was trying this fictional take, and he was ready with factual details for every quandary I encountered. A high point in our joint researches was a six-day retreat we shared at Saint Beuno's, seeing firsthand the holy ground Hopkins so loved.

The first readers of these pages were my wife, Bo Caldwell, whose own gifts as a novelist increased the clarity and accessibility of my prose, and my old friend, Jim Shepard, whose humor, intelligence, insights, and suggestions I could not do without.

To all of these, my thanks.